Good Girl, Bad Guy

By

Ben E. Lewis & Luciana Santiago

ISBN-13:978-1500286873

ISBN-10:1500286877

Dedication

This book is dedicated to our children Kandice, Krystal, Kimani, Osiris, Bennie, and London

Table of Contents

Preface

A modern love saga about two young lovers, whose
consummate attraction for each other leads to a
passionate relationship filled with unconditional love,
personal pains, soul searching, and undeniable desire.
In a world that offers limitless options for individuals,
these two young people have decided to embark upon
a lifetime journey of happiness and sorrow, joy and
pain, truth and deceit, for better or worse, together.

Introduction

When two people are in love with each other, a trusting and committed friendship is usually the foundation of that love. Two strangers meet have a mental and physical connection, then establish a personal bond. Love is supposed to be the highest level of human emotion. Love is supposed to conquer all things bad and bring peace and harmony to all. Love is the epitome of everything good.

However there is an old saying, "There is a thin line between love and hate". Sometimes love can be toxic, and hurtful. Two people that love each other could one day hate each other with the same passion. Love can get ugly, love can be hurtful. Love that was once so beautiful can turn into dark expressions of the human soul. Love can be so intoxicating, that it can blind a person to reality.

Giovanna and Dre are two people in love. Giovanna loves Dre more than she loves herself. Dre loves Giovanna more than life itself. This is their story of how a love so strong, so intense, and so unyielding takes them on a roller coaster ride of life. The bond between Giovanna and Dre will be tested by family and friends. Temptation, jealousy, greed, and envy will also test the strength of their love. In spite of everything that threatens the relationship of Giovanna and Dre they remain deeply in love with each other, and that is the only thing that ultimately matters to them. They made a commitment for life and nothing or nobody can break the attraction that they have for each other.

Giovanna is the good girl from the suburbs. She wants all that life has to offer and she will work harder than anyone to achieve success. Dre is the bad guy from the neighborhood. He is the black sheep of his family that never lived up to the high expectations they once had for him. When the good girl Giovanna meets the bad guy Dre, they had no idea that their ultimate destiny was to love each other for the rest of their lives. This is their story.

Chapter One: "The lovers meet"

It was a slow night at the Pink Slip. The Pink Slip is the most popular urban strip club in St. Louis. Strippers from across the Midwest travel to St. Louis to make some easy, fast money on the weekend. Every night at the Pink Slip professional athletes, entertainers, street hustlers, and hard working men spend money freely, on the beautiful ladies that dance there. Giovanna has been working at the Pink Slip on the weekends for most of the summer. She is not as popular amongst the other dancers because she usually makes more money on weekends than the other girls that work everyday. Giovanna is however, one of the most popular dancers among the male patrons of the Pink Slip. Giovanna has loyal fans that usually leave the club after one drink, if she was not working.

Giovanna was ready to hit the stage for her last dance of the night when she saw a couple of men, enter the half empty club. She immediately recognized one of the new club patrons. He was Smooth, the former director of her neighborhood community center. Giovanna had known Smooth since she was a young teenager. He had always been known as a ladies man by the girls at the community center. He was tall like a basketball player, light-skinned with green eyes. The other man with Smooth she did not recognize. In the dark club the only thing she really noticed about the other man was that he was not as tall as Smooth. Giovanna did notice that he was wearing a Coogi sweater with a Dobbs hat and some Versace glasses. "Typical drug dealer", thought Giovanna.

Smooth and his friend ordered some drinks at the bar, while Giovanna began her final dance routine for the evening. Most of the dancers play loud, bass-thumping, down South rap music when they danced. Giovanna immediately changes the vibe of the club with her favorite song to dance to, "Sweet Dreams". This is another reason the other dancers do not like Giovanna, she never performs to rap music. In the minds of the other dancers, Giovanna thinks she is better than everyone else. Every time Giovanna dances, it rains money in the club. Giovanna made more money half of the way into her dance, than the other previous two dancers combined. As her routine ended and Giovanna gathered all of her tips, Smooth approached the stage. He wanted to tip her directly and Smooth also told Giovanna how good she looked. Giovanna looked directly at Smooth and could tell he had been drinking. "Smooth!" Giovanna exclaimed. "It's me, Giovanna". Smooth focused his eyes, recognized her face and said, "Little Gia, what the hell you in here dancing for?" Giovanna told Smooth to give her a minute to count her money; she would then come back and talk to him.

Gia went to the dressing room to count her money. She separated the dollar bills from the other money, counted out $800 and felt some disappointment. "I can't believe I made less than a thousand", thought Giovanna. Gia felt if she did not make at least a thousand dollars when she danced, it was not worth her time and effort. Gia stashed her money in her bag, changed clothes and went back to talk to Smooth. When she sat at the table with Smooth and his friend, she could tell that they both had been drinking heavily. Smooth immediately asked Gia if she would like to work for him and his cousin at their club. Gia replied, "Smooth you have always been like a big brother to me. I appreciate it but, I'm cool". While Gia and Smooth continued to converse, she noticed that the other man with Smooth just stared at her saying nothing. Smooth finally introduced the two, "Gia this is my cousin Dre. Dre this is Gia, I've known her since she was a little kid back in the day when I worked at the community center." They spoke cordially to each other and Smooth excused himself from the table to go to the bathroom.

Dre had been checking Gia out the entire time he had been at the club. He immediately thought that she was the most beautiful girl at the Pink Slip. While she was dancing to "Sweet Dreams", he became intoxicated with her beauty. Giovanna was tall with an athletic body, like she played basketball or volleyball in high school. She had long natural flowing hair, smooth caramel complexioned flawless skin, mesmerizing Betty Davis eyes, long athletic legs, six-pack belly, and enough ass that it wasn't too ghetto but still made Dre think, "Damn!" Dre watched all the other men at the strip club rain money on Giovanna. Dre was a firm believer that if he was going to tip a stripper, she had to dance for him specifically. Otherwise he let the other guys trick on the ladies while he spends money at the bar. Dre wanted to approach Giovanna about getting a private dance after she finished her routine. However his cousin Smooth had told him that he already knew Gia and she was going to come to the table and talk to him. Dre knew that his cousin Smooth was the closest thing to a pimp without actually having girls on the corner selling sex. Dre assumed that Smooth was about to add Giovanna to his stable of women and she would be soon working at their club.

After Smooth finally introduced Dre and Giovanna, Dre really did not care to pursue her because he thought his cousin Smooth had already hooked up with Gia. When Smooth left Giovanna and Dre alone there was a moment of awkward silence before Dre finally spoke. "Why did you dance to Sweet Dreams? Most strippers dance to booty shaking

11

music," Dre stated. Gia replied confidently, "I'm not a stripper, I'm a dancer. I will dance to whatever song I choose." Dre responded, "I did not tip you for your dance. Next time dance to something more crunk." Gia now obviously annoyed by Dre, began to get up and leave the table. Before she walked away she let Dre know, "I didn't ask you to tip me for my dance, nor did I need you to tip me for my dance." Gia headed back to the dressing room thinking about Dre, "What an asshole". She crossed paths with Smooth, spoke with him briefly and continued to the dressing room.

Upon entering the dressing room Gia noticed someone had gone through her personal belongings. She immediately gathered up her things and made a quick inventory of everything she was supposed to have. Gia immediately noticed a couple of her outfits were missing and all of her dollar bills were gone. She maintained her composure but was sure to let all the girls in the dressing room know her feelings. Giovanna exclaimed for all to hear, "Whoever went through my shit can keep those outfits! If you wanted them that bad just ask I would have gave them to you! I only wear my shit once anyway! You broke bitches can have my dollar bills too! I'm still walking out of this bitch with more money than any of you hoes!"

Smooth and Dre were leaving the club and Dre asked about Giovanna. "What's up with that girl Gia cuz?" Is she gonna work for us?" Dre inquired. Smooth replied, "Yeah man, I'm going to set up an audition for her real soon." Dre had mixed emotions about Smooth's response. Dre had felt an immediate attraction for Giovanna when he met her. He not only thought she was the most beautiful girl in the club, she was the most beautiful woman, Dre had ever laid eyes upon. It was more than Giovanna's physical beauty that attracted Dre. Her quick responses to his arrogant attitude and her confident, independent personality were an instant attraction for Dre as well.

Giovanna left the club that night disappointed that she didn't make enough money, upset that some thirsty bitches had stolen from her, but strongly focused to keep her eye on the prize. Giovanna has a philosophy she calls, "In it to win it." She never lets anything bring her down or hold her back. She briefly ponders over Smooth's offer to work at his club, but she can't get her mind off of his asshole cousin Dre either. "That dude was a straight asshole", thought Gia. Gia also felt a strange attraction to the only guy at the club that didn't tip her.

Chapter Two: "Love is in the air"

Summer was coming to an end and the lives of Giovanna and Dre had kept moving along their separate paths. Gia continued to dance on the weekends and was anticipating the beginning of the fall semester at her college. She had saved enough money to move out of her mother's house and take care of other personal business. Her baby's father was in the county jail and she was determined to help with his bond. Life is supposed to be hard for a teenage mother, but Giovanna is the type of woman that faces life challenges with a supreme confidence to succeed. Dre had stopped working at his cousin's strip club and started his own business. He started a local rap magazine, and his first promotion was a calendar that showcased local models. Dre had gotten bored with the late nights and the constant getting high and drinking that is associated with working at a strip club. He had majored in English when he attended college, and he was a writer for his school annual and newspaper. Dre always wanted to operate his own business, so magazine publishing was a natural choice to use his journalism ability. Destiny had again placed lives of Giovanna and Dre on a path to meet, at an intersection of success and determination.

Gia no longer danced at the strip club. Gia had begun working at a private after-hours club where the owner had made her a featured entertainer. She preferred the private club for several practical reasons. The private club had an exclusive clientele which Gia preferred over the random men that walk into the strip club. Gia was paid a salary plus her tips, since she was a featured dancer at the private club. Some nights Gia would not even dance, she would just walk around and have conversations with club members. Her conversation alone compelled men to want to give Giovanna their money. Giovanna was often propositioned by different men at the private club. Once, a professional basketball player offered her $25,000 to sleep with him. Gia politely declined and referred him to a girl that would sleep with him for $2,500. Gia took the $2,500 from the baller, and gave the other girl $500 to sleep with him. She just made $2,000 for hooking him up with a piece of ass. Easy money moves like this played well with Giovanna's philosophy of, "in it to win it". It was well known at the after-hours club that no matter how much money you had, Gia was there to sell you a dream, not sex. The dream of Gia became expensive for lots of men.

Gia had arrived at the after-hours club and was preparing for another night of getting her money, when she noticed a flyer at the DJ booth. The flyer was promoting a calendar that was being produced by a local rap magazine. Gia was familiar with the magazine and thought that this calendar could possibly be an opportunity for her to expand her credentials into modeling. Even though it was after midnight, she called the contact number on the flyer to get more details about the calendar. To her surprise, even though it was after regular business hours, someone answered the phone. Gia spoke with the laid back voiced man about the calendar and he proceeded to answer all the many questions she had for him. After finishing their conversation, the man that had talked to Gia realized he never got a name or contact number, of the potential model for his calendar. Dre would not have to wait long before he talked to the mystery model again.

Dre's cell phone rang early in the morning and the sweetest voice he ever heard spoke to him. "Can I still be featured in your calendar?" the soft voice asked Dre. "Who is this and why are you calling me so early in the morning?" a groggy Dre replied. "I talked to you last night and you told me to call you back about being featured in your calendar. I want to be on the cover," a confident Gia replied. "Who is this?" Dre perplexingly asked again. "My name is Giovanna, you are going to feature me in your calendar and I am going to be your cover model." Gia stated with confidence. Dre wiped the sleep from his eyes and made his way to the bathroom for the morning piss. While standing at the toilet

Dre responded, "Giovanna, that is a unique name, I have never met anyone with that name before. What is your real name?" Giovanna replied in her most angelic baby voice, "That is my real name. That is the name that my mother blessed me with." After finally gathering his early morning faculties, Dre pondered, "If the voice and name are this sweet, the rest of the package must be outstanding!" Gia interrupted Dre's thoughts and asked him, "To whom am I speaking with and what role do you have with producing the calendar." Dre instantly put on his C.E.O. hat and proceeded to explain to Giovanna that he was the owner of the magazine and what his ambitions were with the calendar venture. Gia proceeded to break down her own personal ambitions, for his calendar venture. After an hour long phone discussion, it was agreed that it would be in the best interests of both parties to establish a working relationship. Giovanna and Dre decided to meet face to face, the next day.

That following day, when they were supposed to meet, Giovanna cancelled her meeting with Dre. So they rescheduled for the next day which was subsequently cancelled also. After two cancelled meetings it seemed as if Giovanna and Dre would never meet. Dre had subsequently scheduled an open casting call for potential calendar models, and he personally invited Giovanna to finally meet him there. "Is this casting call going to be open to any and every body?" Giovanna inquired. Dre informed her that it would be open to the general public. Giovanna reluctantly promised she would attend. Over 30 girls, some that were sexy and some that were not, attended the open model call. Dre and the other producers of the calendar were very confident with the 12 ladies they had chosen. However Dre was confused as to why none of the girls were named Giovanna. Dre continued to communicate with Gia on a daily basis with long phone conversations. Gia had become a surrogate advisor for Dre as production for the calendar moved forward. When production of the calendar finished, Dre decided to host a big promotional launch party. Gia was not a part of the calendar venture, but she and Dre maintained a daily phone relationship leading up to the calendar promotional party. The day of the party Dre finally confronted Giovanna, "Who are you really? We have been having great conversations for months now. You have become a real friend to me. You have given me great business advice. We have talked about our personal problems. We have even had nights of talking dirty to each other. Are we going to ever meet or are you just going to keep faking out on meeting me?" Giovanna felt that her integrity was being challenged and asked Dre what time he was leaving for the calendar launch party. She promised Dre, "I don't have a car, but I will ask my friend to bring me by your house so that we can finally meet. I am never fake I just have a busy life."

Dre was dressed for the party and patiently waiting for Giovanna to arrive. It was 20 minutes past the time that he had planned to leave when he heard a knock at his door. Dre looked out of his door and saw a female with her head down looking towards the floor. Dre thought to himself, "Finally, I get to meet the elusive Giovanna." He opened the door and he felt like an angel from heaven had just stepped into his home. Giovanna cautiously walked into Dre's house, looked into his sexy piercing eyes and immediately felt a hot passion envelop her entire body. Dre was black but he looked like he could have some Mexican or Asian in his family somewhere. She looked at Dre shyly trying not to stare lustfully when he said to her, "Nice to finally meet you in person Giovanna. Are you just going to stand there or can I get a hug?" Gia took a step towards Dre, as he took a step towards her. They hugged each other like two lost souls that had been separated at birth.

Dre squeezed Gia and looked caringly into her eyes and said, "Why aren't you smiling. I've been waiting a long time to see you, and I can't stop smiling." Gia replied, "I don't really like to smile." Dre responded, "When you first walked in you flashed a beautiful smile. Are you disappointed in what you see?" Giovanna immediately told Dre,

19

"No, I'm nowhere close to being disappointed. I just don't like to smile." Giovanna was thinking to herself, "If I stay here any longer, I will fuck this man." Dre knew he was late to his party, but he suddenly did not care about it anymore. The only thing racing through his mind was, the next time he will have an opportunity to spend quality time with Giovanna. Giovanna's ride began honking the car horn, signaling she was ready to leave. Giovanna was nowhere near ready to leave Dre. Dre told her, "Don't keep your friend waiting. I am very impressed with what I see. I wish you could go to the party with me." A disappointed Giovanna stated, "I wish I could go too. I'm not dressed to go out though." Dre reassured her, "If you have some time, we can go out tomorrow. I feel like I have known you for a lifetime, but this the first time I have actually met you in person." Gia promised Dre that she would make some time for him the next day. They hugged each other again like they would never see each other again. Gia left feeling like she had just met the man that would be her husband one day. Dre went to the party dreaming about the angel that walked through his front door. Deep in side he knew that his life was about to change forever. Neither one of them realized that, this was not the first time they had met.

Chapter Three: "How deep is your love?"

There is a seven year age difference between Giovanna and Dre, she is19 and he is 26. However, age was just a number for the two lovers. In the months following Gia and Dre's first face to face meeting at his house, they spent all of their free time together. When Gia was not at school or at work, and her kids were in the care of her mother, she was with Dre. When Dre was not working on his magazine or taking care of other business, he was with Gia. The two lovers made regular trips to the movies, dinner dates, comedy shows, breakfast dates, and often times just riding around St. Louis in Dre's car listening to music. When they made love, it was explosive. Every time Gia and Dre made love it was just like the first time. Sex for the two young lovers was exciting, passionate, uninhibited, intense, raw, and totally satisfying. Giovanna and Dre were becoming inseparable. They were best friends whom become lovers.

The winter holiday season was approaching and all of Giovanna's goals were being accomplished. She had signed a lease for a new townhouse that would be available before Christmas. Living at her mother's house with her two kids and two younger brothers' had never been an acceptable living situation for Gia. She looked forward to having Christmas in her own home with her kids. Gia finally got herself another car. Giovanna has always had a car, since her grandfather gave her the first one when she was 15. The father of her kids got her last car impounded by the police when he went to jail. Having a car again made it easier for Gia to get money that she had been missing, because she did not have transportation. Gia could now make trips to Atlanta, Miami, and New York to get that real money she could not get in St. Louis. Gia could now see Dre anytime she wanted, and not just when he came to get her. It was Sunday afternoon, after a weekend money trip to Atlanta, Gia decided to stop by Dre's house so that she could see her man after a long weekend of getting paid.

Dre was watching football with his usual circle of friends, when he heard a knock at the door. "Hey Gia!" A surprised Dre exclaimed as he answered the door. Gia gave Dre a big hug as she entered his house. "How was your trip?" asked Dre. Gia patted her oversized snakeskin Prada bag and winked at Dre, "It was very good." Dre never judged Gia for being a dancer. He understood that the money she needed to get what she wanted could only be made by dancing or selling cocaine. After the game ended, and it was just Dre and Gia chilling, Giovanna noticed some new pictures on his kitchen table. "What are these?" a curious Giovanna asked. "Those are some old pictures I had just gotten developed." Dre responded. Gia skimmed through the pictures and she came upon a photo, which reminded her of someone she had met once before. The photo was of Dre wearing a Coogi sweater, Dobbs hat, and Versace glasses. Gia looked at the picture, then looked at Dre, looked at the picture, looked at Dre again. "You are that asshole from the Pink Slip!" Gia said to Dre. A confused Dre defended himself, "Asshole? What are you talking about? I haven't been to the Pink Slip." Gia asked, "Do you have a cousin named Smooth?" Dre acknowledged that he did. "You are that asshole from the Pink Slip!" Gia again exclaimed. Dre took a moment to think about what Gia was saying to him and then it hit him. "Sweet Dreams! You are the girl that danced to Sweet Dreams!" Dre finally realized what Gia was talking about. "Man I was drunk as shit that night." Dre confesses. "You were also a complete asshole." Gia reiterates. The two look at each other and realize that the first time their lives crossed paths, it was not a happy moment. After a moment of reflecting on their first meeting, Gia and Dre simultaneously laugh out loud. Two people, whom have fallen so deeply in love with each other, just realized they could not stand each other when they initially met. Dre took Gia to his bedroom, played the song "Sweet Dreams", and they made love passionately.

Over the course of the holidays Gia began to pay more attention to something about Dre's activities. She knew and understood that people called him about his magazine constantly. But Gia was beginning to get more and more frustrated that Dre had to often go, "take care of business", during times they planned to spend together. Sometimes canceling dates altogether. His phone regularly rang after midnight, sometimes even early in the morning. Gia loved Dre, but she was beginning to feel second to the "business" that was so important to Dre. It was New Year's Eve and Gia had not seen or heard from Dre all day. She was starting to worry, so she decided to go by his house and check on him. Upon arriving at Dre's house Gia immediately noticed two unfamiliar cars with California license plates parked outside. She had her own key so she let herself into the house. "Dre", Gia called out. No response. She immediately went upstairs, but no one was there. She called out for Dre at the basement door and still no response. "Where the hell is Dre?" Gia pondered. Suddenly, Dre entered the house with two people Gia had never seen before. One of the guys with Dre was a dark-skinned man with a thick beard that looked like he could have been a football player. The other man was short and fat with a long ponytail that looked like he may have been Puerto Rican or Mexican. "Hey baby! Give me a few minutes and I will be right back." Dre said as he kissed

24

Gia on her cheek. All three of them went downstairs into the basement. Gia thought, "Who the hell were they?" It did not go unnoticed to Gia that Dre did not introduce her to the men either. The dark-skinned man was carrying a large cooler and the fat Mexican had a duffle bag. "What the fuck are they doing in the basement?" Gia wondered. Gia went upstairs to the bedroom where she nervously waited for Dre. Her instincts were telling her that some type of drug deal was going down and she began to worry about Dre. After an uncertain wait of 20 minutes Gia heard Dre escorting the men out of the house.

Gia went downstairs to check on Dre. "What's up baby?" Dre said. "You tell me what's up." Gia replied. "It's all good honey. Those were a couple of friends of mine from Cali." Dre explained. Gia could see the duffle bag and cooler that the men were carrying were now sitting in the kitchen. Dre noticed Gia staring at the bag and cooler and asked her, "You want to see what I have in there?" Gia could not restrain her curiosity of wanting to know. "Check this shit out." Dre said excitedly. Dre opened the cooler and in it was two large vacuum sealed bags filled with nuggets of what looked like purple weed. Gia asked, "Is that weed? Is that purple weed?" A smiling Dre told her, "Hell yeah, this is the New Year come up." Dre proceeded to dump out the contents of the duffle bag and 5 bricks wrapped in gray duct tape fell onto the kitchen table.

"This is the regular for the blue-collar people, and the purple is the exclusive for my premium folks." Dre explained to Gia. Gia stood in Dre's kitchen, dazed and confused. All kinds of thoughts raced through her mind about what Dre had just revealed to her. She was trying to process the fact that, the love of her life sold drugs. Gia had believed that Dre was a businessman that was dedicated to the success of his magazine. Now she has just learned that the man she was in love with was hiding a major part of his life. She could not believe that Dre had been selling drugs and she is just now learning about his other "business". As Giovanna stood in Dre's kitchen not believing what she is seeing she suddenly wondered, what other secrets has Dre been keeping from her?

Chapter Four: "Mixed Emotions"

It is the beginning of a new year and Giovanna and Dre are excited for their future. Gia has settled into her new townhouse. She decorated and furnished her two-story accommodations like a model home featured on Martha Stewart. Gia had her Acura Legend customized with new paint, rims, and a sound system. Dre's magazine was steady growing and becoming more successful. Distribution for the magazine had expanded into Chicago, Kansas City, and Omaha. He made regular out-of-town business trips to support the expansion of his business. Dre also began spending most of his free time at Gia's townhouse. He had started to build a bond with Gia's children; the more he spent time at the townhouse. Dre was at Gia's place on such a regular basis that he eventually had a toothbrush in the bathroom and clothes in the closet. They were not technically living together, because Dre still had his house. However, it seemed that the only time Dre went home was to take care of his side business.

On Wednesday nights, Dre now sponsored an open mic night for singers and rappers at a club in East St. Louis. The open mic night had become a popular hump-day party spot. Dre even incorporated Giovanna's mantra of "in it to win it" to help promote the event on the radio and streets. Gia knew that when Dre came home on Wednesday nights, he was usually sloppy drunk from drinking Remy Martin cognac all night. Dre coming home drunk did not bother Gia. He usually put his car keys, money, and pistol on the dresser and passed out in the bed, fully dressed snoring like a grizzly bear. It was the Wednesday night that Dre did not come home that bothered Giovanna. Gia was restless the entire night because she was not cuddled up to Dre. He was not at home. As the sun rose she became nervous that something bad had happened to him. She called Dre incessantly and he never answered his phone. She began to assume the worst, so she turned on the morning news to see if something tragic had happened. She didn't see anything about Dre on the news. So she got her kids ready for pre-school and daycare, increasingly worried about Dre. After Gia sent her kids off to school, she decided to drive by Dre's house to see if he was there. As soon as she got to his block, she saw his car parked in front of his house. "What the fuck!" Gia thought. She had probably called his cell phone 100 times that morning without getting an answer from Dre. Giovanna's feeling of worry quickly turned into feelings of suspicion.

Gia swooped up in her car at Dre's house and before she knew it, she was at the front door knocking. She knocked normally, and no one answered the door. So Gia decided to incorporate the "police knock", and still no answer. Finally a frustrated and angry Gia began kicking on the solid wood front door. "I know you are in there Dre! Tell what ever bitch you got in there I'm coming in! You better open up this goddamn door before I kick it in motherfucka!" Gia yelled loudly while still attempting to kick in the door. Suddenly the door opened and Dre was butt-naked and looking confused. "Who the hell are you in here fucking?" Gia demanded as she stormed into the house, headed straight to the bedroom. Nervous and naked Dre responded, "Nobody." Gia searched through every room and closet, confident she would find a female in the house. "Where's the bitch at Dre? Why is your ass butt-naked?" Gia demanded. "Ain't nobody here Gia! I was getting in the bathtub and I heard my door being kicked in, so I ran downstairs." Dre unconvincingly pleaded with Gia. Gia quickly replied, "That's bullshit Dre, I know you got a bitch in here!" Gia proceeded to check throughout the house, but still not finding anyone. "I've been calling your phone all night and this morning! Why haven't you called me? I thought something bad happened to you." Gia said to Dre. "I was real fucked up and broke my phone. I didn't think I could drive to your house so I came here." Dre explained. Gia seriously doubted the excuse and story Dre was trying to sell her. Dre proceeded to put on a robe while Gia was still patrolling the house. "If it ain't a bitch here now, you had some bitch here last night. Otherwise you would have brought your ass home last night." Gia declared. Dre desperately tried to convince Gia that she was wrong and after about 45 minutes of debate Gia eventually had to leave for a job interview. Dre watched as Gia drove away and as soon as she was out of his sight, he went straight to the basement door. Dre opened the door to his basement and a nervous and naked female appeared. "You said she was scared to come in your basement. Well I was scared as hell while I was in your basement." The unknown female said to Dre. "Hurry up and get your shit. She might come back." Dre said desperately to the female. The female quickly got dressed and left out of Dre's back door. He had her park her car on the block behind his house, precisely for an emergency such as the one he just encountered. Gia drove away fully convinced that she was right about a strange female being at Dre's house. She felt hurt, betrayed, and deceived. This was the first time she shed a tear over Dre.

Ironically as Gia drove away, a classmate from her school had called Gia on her way to her job interview. He was an African exchange student whom always bragged to Gia that he had money, and he would buy her anything she wanted. Gia figured she might as well make the African put his money where his mouth is. Gia thought to herself, "This dude is always telling me I can have anything I want, let's see what I can get." Dre was obviously getting what he wanted, why shouldn't she? She had the African meet her at the mall after her job interview. The African was so excited to be with Gia that he gave her his American Express black card, and told her she can buy whatever she wanted. Gia is a professional shopper, with an eye for exquisite shoes and handbags. She spent over three hours at the mall acquiring Chanel glasses, some snakeskin belts, several pairs of high end stiletto heels, bottles of expensive perfume, and a Movado watch. By the time her shopping spree was over she had charged over $5000 worth of merchandise to the African's credit card. Gia had gotten a natural high from all the shopping she had just done. What really made her shopping spree therapeutic was the fact that Dre was calling her the entire time and she just ignored his calls. The stress of the earlier incident at Dre's house was alleviated by the time Gia had loaded the trunk of her Acura with all her new gifts.

The relationship between Giovanna and Dre became strained. Gia avoided Dre at all costs. Dre continued to pursue her desperately. His guilt ridden conscience would not let him relax until he had a chance to make amends with his precious Gia. Gia received a job offer from a fortune 500 financial company, which she had previously applied and subsequently interviewed. She was excited about the opportunity to work for a successful company. Gia was raised to expect and represent the best in life and all it has to offer. Now that Gia was offered a great job, she knew working at the after-hours club was about to come to an end. She continued to see her new African benefactor, and even told Dre about him to make him jealous. She was not attracted to her African friend physically or mentally. Gia was attracted to what the he could afford her. She missed spending time with her dearest Dre, but she was still hurting from his betrayal of her trust.

Valentine's Day was approaching. Both Gia and Dre were feeling emptiness in their lives. They both missed each other desperately and longed to renew their love affair. Gia finally accepted a phone call from Dre. "Hey baby." An excited Dre said over the phone. Gia was reserved with her response, "Hi." Dre eagerly confessed, "I miss you baby. I'm so sorry for hurting you. Please forgive me." Gia patiently listened as Dre testified to her. "Would you like to spend Valentine's Day with me?" Dre humbly asked. Gia paused and replied, "Sure, why wouldn't I?" Dre responded, "I really wasn't sure Gia. We have not talked or seen each other recently. I miss you Gia and I really want to spend Valentine's Day with you." Gia told Dre, "I miss you too. I would love to spend Valentine's Day with you." Dre proceeded to make arrangements for a special day with Giovanna. When Valentine's Day arrived, Gia looked absolutely fabulous for Dre. Her hair was perfectly styled, her outfit was flawless, and the new perfume she was wearing intoxicated his senses. "Wow Gia, you look fantastic!" Dre exclaimed. Dre had reserved a horse drawn carriage for the two lovers to take on a romantic ride. Following the carriage ride, Dre treated Gia to a three-course dinner complete with a bottle of champagne. After dinner Dre presented Gia a heartfelt, apologetic card and some fine crafted artisan chocolate. Gia was enjoying the day of romance she was sharing with Dre. She wished everyday could be like the fairytale day she was experiencing. Dre was always a gentleman when he was with her, but today he could have wrote a book on chivalry. It was the end of the evening, and it was time for Dre to take Gia home. He let her know how much he enjoyed spending Valentine's Day with her, and hoped that they could begin spending more time together again. Gia sat in the passenger seat of his car, staring at Dre with a fire burning inside of her. "You don't have to take me home yet. We can stop by your house." Gia said seductively. Dre looked at Gia with his piercing eyes and asked, "Are you sure?" Gia looked at him with her sensuous eyes, smiled and nodded her head in assurance. Upon arriving at Dre's house, the two of them immediately embraced in a deep passionate kiss. The magnetism they had for each other had been intensified by the time they had spent apart. The lovers indulged in the mutual pleasure of each other, like wild animals in heat. In the afterglow of their earth-shaking sexual session, as Gia cuddled upon the smooth chest of Dre, she gazed into his eyes and said, "Dre, I love you." Dre stared back at Gia and replied, "I love you to Gia. I'm so sorry that I hurt you. I will never hurt you again." Gia looked at Dre, smiled softly, and the two of them drifted off into peaceful sleep.

Chapter Five: "Stay with me"

Gia and Dre are once again inseparable. As the two reunited lovers slept in a Valentine's Day bliss, Dre was awakened by Gia's persistently ringing cell phone. He woke up his sleeping beauty, so that she could see who was desperately trying to contact her. Gia answered the phone and it was her mother, frantically crying through the phone. "Granddad died tonight! Granddad died baby! Your Granddad is dead Giovanna!" Her mother sadly informed her. Gia dropped her phone and her countenance became a blank stare. A concerned Dre immediately asked, "What's wrong Gia?" Gia was obviously emotionally traumatized, tears began to run down her face and she whispered to Dre, "My Granddad died in his sleep tonight." A quiet calm overcame the room, before Gia began to cry uncontrollably. "No, no, no! Not Granddad!" said a distraught Gia. Attempting to console his devastated soulmate, Dre held Gia tightly and reassured her that he was there to comfort her. Gia quickly got dressed and told Dre, "We need to go to my Granddad's house right now!" Dre raced to Gia's granddad's house and they arrived upon a chaotic scene of devastated family members and busy paramedics.

An emotional Gia was not allowed to enter her grandfather's house while the paramedics were still inside. This angered her, and she lashed out at the people she felt were keeping her from seeing her beloved patriarch. Gia's grandfather had been the most influential man in her life. Her relationship with her biological father was distant, even though they lived in the same city. She had formed a bond with her stepfather, which was broken when he started smoking crack and abusing her mother. Her grandfather had been her rock, her heart, and her soul. He taught her how to drive, how to cook, and he always told her how beautiful she was. They spent a lot of quality time together, watching classic John Wayne and James Bond movies. They had long talks about life and the world around them. Of all the things that Gia learned from her grandfather, she learned the value of education, hard work and making money.

As the paramedics rushed Gia's grandfather away, overlooked in all the confusion was Gia's younger brother Jerome standing by himself just staring into the night. Jerome was fourteen years old, and he had been living with his grandfather. Jerome had been living with his grandfather, so that the elder man would not be home alone. Giovanna and Jerome hugged each other, and then Jerome began to release tears and emotions he had been attempting to hold inside. Jerome confessed to his older sister, "I found Granddad, Sissy." Giovanna's younger brother affectionately referred to her as Sissy. Jerome continued, "I had spent the night at Chad's house and when I came back home, the house had a funky smell. I called out for Granddad, and he never said anything. I went to his room Sissy", Jerome paused and began crying. "Granddad was just lying in his bed Sissy! His body had swollen and he didn't even look like Granddad, but I knew it was him Sissy." The siblings both began crying while hugging and consoling each other during this tragic moment.

Dre had awkwardly retreated to his vehicle, to respect the grieving family. Gia and Jerome walked together towards Dre's car and both entered. Gia introduced Dre to her brother. "This is my younger brother Rome." Dre proceeded to speak with the Gia's brother that she had nicknamed, Rome. "Nice to meet you Lil Rome. I wish we could have met under different circumstances bro." Dre said. "Gia has told me a lot about you, Dre. I'm glad to finally get a chance to meet you to bro." Rome replied. "Dre, did you know that you had half of a blunt in your back seat?" continued Rome. Dre told Rome he could have the blunt if he wanted it, he understood if the young man needed a smoke. "Thanks bro." An appreciative Rome said to Dre, as he proceeded to fire up the weed. Dre took note that Rome could have pocketed the blunt and never said a word to him. Gia's little brother displayed honesty and integrity to Dre, and those were qualities he rarely saw in young people. Dre and Rome had just met, but they naturally referred to each other as bro. Rome respected the fact that his sister loved Dre, and Dre respected the love that Gia had for her brother. A new kinship was formed between the two male figures in Gia's life, that she felt were the most important to her.

Dre, Gia, and Rome left the aftermath of the scene at her grandfather's house. Gia couldn't bear to just sit outside of her grandfather's house, and she wanted to make sure her traumatized younger brother was safe. They drove to Gia's mother's house. All three of them sat outside for a brief moment, reflecting over everything that had just turned the lives of Gia and Rome upside down. Some guys from the neighborhood that were walking down the sidewalk recognized Rome and stopped to talk. Another reason Jerome lived with his grandfather was so that he could be away from the drug dealers and gangs in his mother's neighborhood. Rome talked with the three men and told Gia he was going to walk to the store with them. Gia quickly pulled Rome away from the men and told him, "You need to be here when Momma gets back from the hospital. Don't get your ass down here and start hanging out with these fuckers. They stay in some bullshit."

Rome reassured his sister, "I'm just going to the store Sissy. I will be alright." Gia looked at the three men suspiciously and as Rome walked off with them she told them, "Don't ya'll get my brother caught up in no bullshit. Otherwise ya'll gonna have to answer to me." The men laughed and one of them said, "We won't OG Giovanna." Gia quickly responded, "That's right, I know where all ya'll mommas live."

Gia and Dre watched Rome walk away and it was just the two of them again. "Are you going to be O.K., baby?" Dre asked. "Not really." An obviously sad Gia said to him. "I need to go to the house and take care of some business." Dre reluctantly told Gia. Gia looked Dre directly in the eyes, with the sadness of a child who just learned that Santa was not real. "Don't leave me right now Dre. I'm hurting. It's about to be a bunch of bullshit with my momma's brother and sister about who is getting what in my Granddad's will. My brother just walked off with some niggas, and God only knows what they are about to do. I need your support through this baby." Dre looked back at Gia. He was never good at saying no to Gia. Whatever Gia wanted, Dre did his best to accommodate and provide. Dre stayed with Gia. Giovanna slid into a mild depression behind the death of her beloved Granddad. A supporting Dre insured her kids made it to school on those bad days when Gia was struggling. Dre cooked for Gia when she didn't want to eat. Dre tried to make life as normal as possible for Gia during these dark days. Dre and Gia grew even closer together. He had held her hand and walked with her, through one of the most traumatic experiences she had ever faced. Dre had gotten closer to Gia's family during this period. Her brother Rome was an aspiring rapper and Dre used his connections helped him find some studios and music producers. Gia's mom began calling Dre, her other son. Gia's kids even began calling Dre dad. Gia quickly corrected that situation, because she never wanted her children to be disconnected with their biological father. She simply told the children to call him Dre, even though her intelligent four-year-old always said, "Dre does everything a daddy is supposed to do."

Dre was now officially living with Giovanna and life was settling down to a sense of normalcy for them. Dre let his cousin Big Slim live in his house, so that he could ensure his weed business did not slow down. Dre also stopped his open mic nights at the club. He was growing closer with Rome and becoming more involved in his aspiring rap career. Gia was becoming more secure at her job. She was recognized for perfect attendance and also for meeting and exceeding all performance standards, at the financial service company she worked. Occasionally she would dance at the private after-hours club. Giovanna was well known for her one-of-a-kind dance wardrobe. She had become somewhat of an urban legend because of a pair of stiletto heels she had custom made. The heels were fitted with multi-colored lights and every time she took a step thy lit up brightly. All the dancers and the male customers wanted to know where Giovanna purchased those light-up stilettos, which had only been seen on her feet.

The happiness of Gia and Dre seemed like something out of a storybook. It had been a couple of months since Valentine's Day and the death of Gia's grandfather. One day at work, Gia realized that she hasn't had her period since before that time. She quickly considered her recent weight gain, and her endless craving for hot wings and potato skins. A mild panic overcame Gia so when she took her lunch break, she went directly to a drugstore and purchased a pregnancy test. The test was positive. A multitude of emotions overcame Gia. She was happy then sad, she was excited then worried. The only thing she really was really sure of was that she had to let Dre know immediately.

Chapter Six: "Secrets and rumors"

Gia called Dre to tell him that, she had something important to share with him when she got off work. Dre pondered over various scenarios of what Gia wanted to tell him. "Did she get fired? Was one of his exes working with her? Was she about to tell him he needs to move out of her place?" Dre's warped mind envisioned several reasons why Gia made a special call to let him know she had something to tell him. Dre attempted to relax his nerves by going to the liquor store and buying some beer to go with his blunt. Dre anxiously anticipated Gia's arrival. Rome stopped by and the two of them played the Playstation to pass some time. Big Slim contacted Dre and told him he needs to come by the house as soon as possible. When Gia eventually arrived at their townhouse, Dre met her at the front door. "Hey baby, how was your day?" He asked, as she entered their home. Gia went directly into the kitchen and grabbed a bottle of water out of the refrigerator. She took a sip of the water and looked lovingly at Dre. Gia smiled and placed the pregnancy test on the kitchen counter. Dre looked at the test on the counter, and then he looked puzzled at Gia. "What is that?" Dre asked in disbelief. Gia looked directly at Dre and said, "What do you think it is?" Dre felt a nervous sinking feeling overtake the inside of his stomach. "That looks like a pregnancy test." Dre said. Gia smartly replied, "Congratulations genius, you are correct." A wide-eyed Dre stared at the test and asked, "Are you for real?" Gia smiled at Dre and said, "For real." Dre began to pace back and forth in the kitchen rubbing both hands down his face. Gia looked at his response to the pregnancy news and the smile on her face slowly disappeared. "What are you thinking about Dre? What's on your mind?" Gia asked. Dre quickly snapped, "You are having another baby is on my mind." "Damn, damn, damn" repeated Dre. "What's wrong with that?" Gia asked confidently. Dre quickly pleaded, "You already have two kids. The last thing I wanted to do is put anymore hardship on you by having another baby." Even more confidently Gia responded, "I have a good job with insurance, your business is doing great. We love each other. At least I know that, I love you." Still pacing the floor and now shaking his head Dre did not say anything. "What's wrong Dre?" Gia asked several times with no response. Then Dre stopped pacing the kitchen floor. He looked squarely at Gia and proceeded to reveal to her, "I have a wife and child in Atlanta. I need to go to Atlanta to see if we are going to reconcile, before I put any thought into having a baby with you."

A stunned Giovanna was instantly devastated. She became slightly light-headed and walked out of the kitchen to go sit down on the loveseat in the living room. Thoughts of what Dre just revealed raced through her head, "A wife and child in Atlanta? A motherfuckin wife and child in Atlanta? This punk-ass, lying nigga, has a wife and child in Atlanta?" With a guilt-ridden face, Dre looked at Gia and said weakly, "I'm sorry baby. I didn't want to hurt you with this. I just need to see if I can get my family back together." Gia's devastation transitioned to anger when she heard Dre's weak apology and explanation. Gia exploded on Dre. "Take yo ass to your fucking wife and baby and live happily ever after! I will raise this baby by myself! I don't need you or any other weak ass motherfucka to do shit for me or my kids. I've been doing it by myself and I will continue to do this by myself! Fuck you Dre and the ship you rode in on!" Dre felt his heart drop into his stomach. He looked at Giovanna's face as she killed him with her words. He knew he had fucked up. He knew it was over between him and Giovanna.

Giovanna let Dre gather all of his belongings. She took the key to her house, and watched him walk the green mile from their once happy relationship. Giovanna could not believe the man she had fell so deeply in love with, the man that she was so excited about bringing a new life into the world with, the man that she had become totally devoted to, had been so secretive and insincere with her. First she discovered he sold drugs, now she finds out he has a wife and child in Atlanta. What's the next deep, dark secret Dre is keeping from her? Gia desired to raise a family and be with Dre forever. However, the reality of her situation was dictating that she was about to continue to live her life as a single parent. Gia did not see Dre again until it was time for her baby to be born. It was hard for her to move forward, while her past was still an important part of her present. Dre never reconciled with his wife. He received divorce papers two days after Gia had told him she was pregnant.

During the time of Gia's pregnancy Dre overindulged in weed, alcohol, and late night partying. He spent most of his time with his cousin Smooth and his other cousin recently released from prison, CJ. After Dre moved back into his house, he had to adjust to having a roommate, his cousin Big Slim. Big Slim had children with four different women and on any given night one of them would be spending the night at the house, Dre now shared with Big Slim. Dre was not accustomed to so many different people invading his private space. Dre neglected his magazine business, and his weed business did not seem to make much money either. More than likely it was due to the fact that

Dre was supplying daily weed smoke-outs with Big Slim, to all the different women that paid a visit to their house. When Dre spent time with his cousin CJ, it was usually at some of the same music studios, where he took Lil Rome. CJ was on parole and could not smoke weed, but that did not stop him and Dre from downing bottles of Hennessy and Remy Martin every time they got together. Smooth tried to get Dre's mind off of Gia by introducing him to new women. Smooth always kept a stable of sexy ladies and he thought that the best way get the monkey off of Dre's back, was by having one of his bitches take his mind off of his troubles. Despite all of the distractions that were now apart of Dre's life, he thought about Gia everyday. Dre missed Gia badly. Dre desperately wanted the life that he had with Gia, again. The devil seemed to attack Dre from all angles while he was apart from Giovanna. His sister had called and told him that a guy she went to high school with was claiming to be the father of Giovanna's baby. Dre did not care, he still missed Gia. One of Smooth's women told Dre that she heard Gia was selling sex at an after-hours club. Dre did not believe the accusation, but if it was true he still did not care. In spite of all the distractions, rumors, and accusations, Dre missed Gia, wanted to make amends to Gia, and if it was the will of God, he wanted to be in a relationship with Gia. Dre loved Gia, and the only person he could blame for the hurt he had caused her, was himself. Dre looked in the mirror and did not like the person he saw.

While Dre was living in a world of guilt and self-pity, Gia was working hard and preparing for the birth of her child. She ate healthy, exercised and never let herself get down about the situation she found herself in. She still had her African benefactor that provided her with financial resources. Despite the fact that the only physical contact she ever had with him was holding hands, he willingly showered her with gifts. The only thing the African man did receive was the fact that he could take Gia around his friends and family and show-off his beautiful "girlfriend". Giovanna also had developed a supportive relationship with a guy she knew from her high school days. This old friend took over Dre's responsibility of ensuring that Gia went to her doctor visits, and provided her with an emotional outlet during her pregnancy. The friend from high school even went as far as to claim Gia's baby as his own, since Dre had not been handling his responsibilities. In spite of the support Gia was receiving financially and emotionally from other men, she would have rather had Dre by her side for her pregnancy. Despite the hurt, pain, and lies that Dre brought upon Gia, she missed him and wished things were like they were before. Giovanna always thought about a saying her grandfather had, "You can't help who you love."

Chapter Seven: "A new beginning"

The due date for Gia and Dre's baby had arrived. Dre was at home smoking and drinking with his cousin Big Slim, when his phone rang. "Hey Dre, I'm just calling to tell you that I'm at the hospital about to have my baby and you can come here if you want." The calm voiced Gia said. Dre eagerly responded, "I'll be up there Gia, I'm on my way!" Gia replied, "Ok, you don't have to come. I just wanted to let you know that I was about to have my baby. Bye." Dre sensed a bit of animosity in Gia's voice. He also noticed how she referred to the baby as hers and not theirs. Big Slim offered to take Dre to the hospital. They rode together in Big Slim's truck and Dre was obviously nervous. "What is the matter with you, aren't you happy about the baby?" Big Slim asked Dre. "Man I haven't been there at all for Gia, throughout her pregnancy. I really didn't think that I would ever hear or see from her again. When I answered the phone and heard her voice, I felt like she was giving me an opportunity to be a father to my child." Dre said. Dre then thought to himself, "Gia didn't have to call me, I'm so glad she did. All I want to do is be an important part of my child's life and try to keep a cordial relationship with Gia." When Dre and Big Slim arrived at the hospital Gia had already given birth. Dre looked at his healthy newborn son in the hospital nursery and a sense of pride overcame him, as it does most new fathers. He told Big Slim that he could leave. Dre was going to stay with Gia and his son until they were released from the hospital.

When Gia saw Dre walking into her recovery room, she naturally smiled at him. Dre smiled back. "He's so beautiful." Gia said. "I know." Dre responded. Dre added, "What is his name? I didn't see a name on his crib." Gia looked at Dre slyly, "I'm thinking about naming him Kunta." A puzzled Dre looked at her and said, "Kunta? What kind of name is that? I want to name him after me." Gia paused and said to Dre, "Why should I name him after you? He's my baby. I carried him by myself and I had him by myself." A feeling of guilt overcame Dre, after Gia's declaration. He sat quietly for a moment and pleaded with her, "Gia, I know you have carried the load by yourself. There is nothing I can do to change that. I really want to be an important part of my first-born son's life. My dad was not a part of my life and I don't want my son to go through life without his father there for him." Gia then reminded Dre, "What about your wife and child in Atlanta? What are you going to do about them? Dre quickly responded, "She has moved on with her life. I'm so, so, so sorry about how I dropped that on you Gia. It was not fair to you and I deserved all of the bullshit that I've had to deal with since. My life is shit right now Gia. I miss you, I was so glad when you called me!" Gia looked at Dre suspiciously and told him, "I just called, so that you could see your child, if you wanted. I didn't call you to get back together with you. We now have a child together and this was a test to see if you wanted to be a part of your child's life." Dre said, "I do want to be a part of our child's life. I want to be a better dad for my son, than my dad was for me. However, I really don't want my son's name to be Kunta." Gia looked directly at Dre and asked, "Well, what do you want to name him?" Confidently Dre said, "I want to name him after me, of course." Gia toyed with Dre a bit, "I don't know about that Dre, I like Kunta. The world might not be ready for another Dre. Let me think about it." Dre and Gia continued to sit and talk while they were in her recovery room. It had been months since they had seen each other and it was an opportunity for them to clear the air.

Gia told Dre about her African benefactor and friend from high school, and how they were there for her throughout the pregnancy. Dre told Gia that he really hasn't done anything with his life except drinking and smoking weed. He told her about the guilt he has felt for not being there through her pregnancy. Gia let Dre know that she could smell alcohol and weed on him when he entered the hospital room. Nevertheless, she was surprised and happy to see him. After an hour of talking and even sharing some laughs with each other, a nurse interrupted the impromptu reunion. "Have you settled on a name for your beautiful little boy?" The nurse asked Gia. Gia looked at Dre then turned to the nurse and said, "Yes. I'm going to name him Dre, after his father." An excited Dre jumped out of his seat pumping his fist in the air. "Yes!" he exclaimed. Dre looked at Gia and held her hand. "Thank you Gia. I really wanted my first-born son to be named after me. From the bottom of my heart, I thank you." Gia looked at Dre and jokingly said, "Well, I'm glad you made it here to see your child. I didn't think you would come to the hospital. If you would not have come to the hospital, I was really going to name the baby, Kunta." Dre looked at Gia and responded, "Damn, that would be fucked up." With a serious look, Gia told Dre, "I'm going to give you a chance to be a father to your child. I would never try to keep your child away from you. Now just because you have a chance to be in your child's life, does not mean I am inviting you back into my life." Dre replied, "I appreciated that Gia. I am going to be the best father in the world. Thank you Gia." The nurse entered the room again with the newly named baby. Gia looked at Dre and said, "Why don't you hold your son." Dre picked up his newborn son and looked into his fresh face. Dre looked at Gia and thanked her again. He preceded to hand the baby to his mother and stood there smiling as the child began to nurse. Dre thought to himself, "This is what I want, a family." Dre knew in his heart that he still loved his precious Giovanna. Giovanna was overcome by feelings in her recovery room, which she has not felt in a long time. She looked at Dre while she was nursing the baby and felt a sense of happiness. Giovanna knew in her heart, that in spite of everything, she still loved her darling Dre.

The birth of little Dre had brought the lives of Giovanna and Dre back together. Dre was a reliable, supportive, and loving father. Giovanna had returned back to work and quickly lost the weight she had gained during pregnancy. Gia was happy that Dre was such a wonderful father, and she appreciated the fact that he was an on-hand parent. They had formed a practical co-parenting relationship that worked to the benefit of both parents. The new responsibility of fatherhood brought about some significant changes in Dre's lifestyle. His cousin, Big Slim, moved out of his house and all of the late night partying soon ended. Dre focused on his lagging business. He produced a rap compilation album that featured various up and coming artists from St. Louis. Gia's brother Lil Rome and Dre's cousin CJ were prominently featured on the album. Dre had planned on producing solo albums for CJ and Rome on his newly formed independent record label. Life was beginning to become exciting again for Dre. Gia began to cautiously open her heart to Dre again. She was delighted with the fact that Dre was such a wonderful dad to his child, and her other children. She supported him with his new record label endeavor. The fact that Dre was helping her younger brother live his dream of being a rapper meant a lot to Gia. Gia never forgot the heartache and pain Dre had caused her, but she really appreciated the man that he had now become. Gia and Dre began to occasionally date again, as a family. They took family outings to the amusement park, Harlem Globetrotters, and the movies. Dre truly cherished these moments he had with Gia. Gia began to look forward to the times she would spend with Dre.

It was the Sunday afternoon, after Gia and Dre had finished a family dinner at her mother's house, when their hearts would collide again. Giovanna's mother was a loving Rastafarian woman that adored Dre. She referred to Dre as her son, and she was glad that he was a part of Giovanna and her family's life. After the family feast, Giovanna's mother suggested that her and Dre take a break from the kids and enjoy a night out together. Dre eagerly agreed, however Gia was reluctant to leave the responsibility of the kids on her mother. "Go ahead and have a night on the town pumpkin. The babies will be just fine with me. I don't mind at all." Gia's mother reassured her. A hesitant Gia decided to take her mother's advice and she confirmed the plans for the evening with Dre.

"There is a new movie I would like to go see." Gia informed Dre. "I need to go home and change first." Gia also told him. Gia went to her house, accompanied by Dre and changed her clothes for their night out. Dre patiently waited for her, eager to have some one on one time with Gia. When Gia was finally satisfied with the outfit she chose for the evening, she entered the room and simply hypnotized Dre with her beauty. Dre stared at the stunning Gia as she wore a form fitting black and white skirt, black Armani shirt, and white and black stiletto heels. "Wow you look amazing!" An impressed Dre said. "You think so? I just threw this outfit together." Gia said nonchalantly. They proceeded to have an enjoyable evening at the movies, and decided to stop at a bar and grill for some late night cocktails. Dre kept telling Gia what a wonderful time he was having and how beautiful she looked. Gia also enjoyed the time she was spending with Dre and was beginning to rekindle feelings she thought were buried. As it began to get late in the evening Gia, called her mother to let her know she was coming to get her babies. Gia's mother answered the phone and told Gia, "Don't worry about the babies pumpkin, they are all sound asleep. You can come and pick them up in the morning." Gia began to wonder, "Was my mother up to something?" Gia suspected that her mother was trying to play cupid, and give her and Dre time alone together. If that was the case the plan was working.

Dre and Gia finished off their drinks and began the drive back to Gia's house. "I had a wonderful time with you tonight, baby." Dre said to Gia. She looked at Dre and said. "I had a great time too. You know you just called me baby?" Dre apologized, "I'm sorry. I was feeling comfortable and relaxed, it just came out." Gia told Dre, "You don't have to apologize. I miss you calling me baby." Dre turned and stared at Gia, as she turned and gazed at him. Dre then stated, "You will always be my baby Gia. No matter what happens in our lives, I will always love you. You are an angel in my life, and I just appreciate the time that I do get to spend with you." Gia smiled lovingly at Dre and said, "Thank you. That meant a lot to me. I don't know what it is Dre, but I just can't stop loving you." Gia then told Dre, "You don't have to take me home, if you don't want to." Curiously, Dre looked at Gia and asked, "What do you want to do? I can't think of anywhere else we can go." Gia looked at Dre with a devious smile, "I'm sure you can think of somewhere we can go." Nervously Dre suggested, "Would you like to go to my house?" Gia smiled and nodded her head in approval. They arrived at Dre's house and consummated a passionate relationship that refused to stay dormant. Gia and Dre made sweet love until the birds began singing and the sun rose to shine light on a new day, and a new beginning.

Chapter Eight: "The good life"

The afterglow of a night of passion was evident on the faces of Gia and Dre. They picked up the children from Gia's mom, and then went their separate ways to individual daily routines. Dre had a studio session with Lil Rome, and Gia had to be at work. Over the course of the next few months, leading up to little Dre's first birthday the couple rekindled a love affair that refused to be extinguished.

Dre had once again begun to spend more time at Gia's townhouse. When he had to be at his house, Gia was usually right there with her man. Since Gia was aware of Dre's weed business, he is not as secretive as he once was. She even occasionally took him on his weed runs. He truly did not want to expose Gia to that side of his life, but the cat was already out of the bag. Dre and Gia were also regular fixtures on the urban social scene in St. Louis. Dre had begun promoting concerts that brought in national headlining acts with local artists usually opening the show. Gia always worked at the front door of the concert venue, to ensure safekeeping and an accurate accounting of ticket sales. Gia and Dre were quickly becoming known as the Jay & Beyonce couple around the St. Louis urban social scene. In addition to the magazine publishing and concert promotion ventures, they often received V.I.P. treatment at nightclubs, comedy shows, and restaurant grand opening celebrations. Gia had a reputation as a fashion trendsetter in St. Louis. Whenever she was out on the town, she always stood out from the crowd with her trademark heels, expensive jewelry, and never duplicated, often imitated wardrobe. Life was good for Gia and Dre.

Dre was also working hard producing the upcoming album for Gia's brother, Lil Rome. The album Dre had produced for his cousin CJ was a good album, but it served more as a music business teaching tool for Dre. Dre learned that it was hard to sell an album without a song being played in the clubs or on the radio. Lil Rome had a song that was getting some radio play and being heard in the clubs around St. Louis. The local hit record by Lil Rome was going to push the album sales that Dre needed, in order to validate his record label. Dre decided to invest in a video for Lil Rome, to further support his hit song. Gia coordinated the video shoot for Lil Rome. They worked as a team to ensure a smooth production of the video. When it was time for the release of Lil Rome's album, anticipation for it was peaking. The song had become a local favorite, and the video provided even more exposure. Dre decided to have a big album release celebration for Lil Rome at the most popular music store in St. Louis. There were free hot dogs, a marching band, and the local radio station did a live broadcast during the event. All of the promotion and marketing to support Lil Rome's debut album, led to the album being the top seller in St. Louis. Dre's record label has established itself as successful. Lil Rome was the most popular local rapper in St. Louis, Gia was the glue that kept everyone together, and life was good.

In the midst of the positive changes and successful ventures in Dre's life, there was one aspect of his life that began to concern him. The fact that he and Gia had separate residences began to represent only a partial commitment to their relationship, in Dre's mind. In Dre's mind, if he and Gia were going to be fully committed to each other, they only needed one residence. Gia however viewed them having separate residences totally different. She was an independent woman. Her and Dre may have a child together and occasionally spend extended periods of time at each other's home, but her townhouse was her own personal sanctuary. If she needed space from Dre or if things got a bit rocky, she always had somewhere she could lay her head and call her own. Dre had a history of fucking up, and Gia did not want to end up in a situation where she had nowhere to go. They were not married, so Gia felt it was the best to maintain her own residence. Dre wanted to fall asleep and awake with Gia by his side, everyday of his life.

As Gia and Dre were lying in her bed watching TV together, Dre decided to bring the subject of their living arrangements to the forefront of their lives. "Gia, why don't you and the kids move in with me?" Dre asked. Gia paused a moment and with a deliberate response she said, "I like my place. Besides, I don't want to bring the kids around all of the extra activities you have going on there." Dre then suggested, "I can shut that shit down immediately. It's more space at my house for all your clothes and shoes, and the kids would have a more room too." An unconvinced Gia asked Dre, "Why all of a sudden do you want me to move in?" Dre stated, "I love you Gia, and I want to fall asleep and wake up with you everyday." Gia countered, "We do that now." A determined Dre reasoned, "I know baby, but I think that if we all lived together it would be better for us." Still unconvinced Gia jokingly said, "Dre, you just want me to move in, so you can have me on lockdown." Now laughing Dre responded, "Okay I admit, I just want to have you all to myself. I just want us to be together forever." Gia smartly responded, "You sound like you want to get married or something." The subject of marriage made Dre withdraw from the conversation about them moving in together. Gia would not let him back out easily. "What's the matter Dre, you got all quiet and shy when I brought up marriage. You want me to move in with you, but you are not ready to even talk about getting married." Dre quickly countered, "Could you see yourself married to me, Gia?" Gia replied, "Well you have to ask me and find out." Dre got quiet again until Gia added, "I'm not going to make any quick decision, but I will think about us living together." Dre smiled and they both continued to watch television.

Suddenly, there was a loud knock on Gia's front door. Dre hopped out of the bed to see who the unexpected visitor was. It was a friend of Lil Rome, with a look of distress on his face. "Lil Rome is high and out of control. He's kicking cars and fighting a tree!" The friend told Dre. Gia had followed Dre down the stairs, and they both went ran with the friend to help Lil Rome. When they came upon him, he was totally out of control. He was yelling unintelligible words and punching a tree, they saw several damaged cars that he apparently had caused. "What the hell is wrong with him?" Gia asked the friend. "Lil Rome smoked a dip and he can't handle it." Dre immediately knew that smoking a PCP dipped cigarette could make a person temporarily insane and hallucinate. They tried to subdue him but he was too strong. Gia finally pulled the big sister card and grabbed her brother, looked him directly in the eyes and said, "I don't know what your damn problem is, but you have to calm down right now!" Lil Rome looked back at his sister and began crying uncontrollably. By now a crowd had gathered and a fast approaching police siren could be heard in the distance. Dre and Gia guided a disoriented Rome back to Gia's house so that he would not get arrested and so he could come down from his bad PCP trip. The police ended up knocking on Gia's door looking for Lil Rome. She denied he was there and since they did not have a search warrant, she refused to let them enter. Gia sat with her brother until he finally began to calm to and come down from his PCP induced hysteria. As soon as Rome exhibited some coherency, Gia immediately chastised him, "What the hell are you smoking dips for Jerome?" Are you trying to literally lose your mind?" Rome pleaded his case, "I didn't know I was smoking a dip sissy. I wouldn't have smoked it if I knew what it was." Gia reminded Rome, "I told you about hanging out with those niggas. If they were really your friends, they wouldn't have let you smoke that bullshit." Rome did not appreciate being lectured by his sister. Dre quietly stayed in the background, while the siblings sorted out the situation.

Gia continued to chastise her brother, "One day you are gonna learn. Those niggas don't give a damn about you. You got a little hood fame from your music, that's the only reason they fuck with you now. I'm telling you Jerome, you better watch your front and back if you gonna keep fucking with them." Rome mumbled under his breath and half-heartedly agreed with what his sister was saying to him. "Does

63

momma know about what happened sissy?" Rome asked. Gia confirmed, "Hell yeah, somebody is going to have to pay for the damage you did to those cars." Rome's head fell in disappointment. He thanked his sister and told Dre he would see him later. Rome left her home embarrassed and ashamed as he walked to his mother's house. Even though he avoided being arrested by the police, Rome would suffer consequences and repercussions for his actions while he was high on PCP. A week after his psychotic episode, his mother received an eviction letter from her landlord. The owners of the vehicles whose cars were damaged had reported the incident to the property manager. Following an internal investigation, it was determined that Rome was under the influence of drugs, and there was zero tolerance for drug activity. Therefore Gia's mom was now being evicted from her home because of the actions of her brother.

The eviction notice for Gia's mom to vacate the premises was ten days. She tried to help her mother find another place to live within the ten day period, but her efforts were fruitless. Dre was feeling the pressure that Gia was under, trying to help her mother relocate. He had a solution that could possibly ease that pressure. Dre suggested that Gia's mom and brothers stay with him temporarily until they found somewhere permanent. Gia was reluctant to do that. She couldn't put her family off on him like that. Dre then offered his place to Gia and her mom, and he could just stay at her townhouse. Gia did not like that idea either. Finally, with no other choice Giovanna told Dre that she would move in with him, while her mom and brothers also looked for another place. Dre was excited about Gia moving in, but at the same time he had reservations about her mom and brothers moving in as well. Nevertheless he was determined to make it work. After all it was only a temporary arrangement, for her mother and brothers. Gia dipped into her savings and paid a years' rent at her townhouse in advance. She was moving in with Dre, but she was going to keep her townhouse as an insurance policy, if their living arrangements did not work. Gia's mother did find another place to live, after a month and a half of the entire family living together. Once Gia helped her mother settle in her new place, the reality of her and Dre living together began to sink in. This was the first time she has ever lived with a man. She wasn't married to Dre, but now they were "playing house". Gia was not sure how her new living situation would work. She figured now that she has made this drastic move, she might as well make the best of the situation. She loved Dre, he loved her, they were a winning team, and she was in it to win it.

Chapter Nine: "Trouble in paradise"

Living with Dre was a joyful experience for Giovanna. Gia relished the opportunity to put a woman's touch on his bachelor pad. She enjoyed preparing meals for her family, as well as hosting family gatherings at their house. It was at these gatherings that Gia discovered that not everyone in Dre's family was happy to see them together. Gia's mother loved Dre dearly, and extended her blessings to their relationship. However Dre's mother, sister, and several of his female cousins did not exactly extend that same acceptance and hospitality to Gia. Gia was under the impression that Dre's family was happy he had finally settled down with one woman. However, when Dre, Gia and the kids attended several holiday family gatherings, his family often gave everyone but Dre the cold shoulder. Eventually Gia stopped going to his family affairs, she was tired of dealing with fake smiles and phony friendships. Dre also noticed how his family often whispered and gossiped about Gia. Some of the females in his family even went as far as accusing Gia of being seen with other men. Dre grew increasingly frustrated with the way his family treated the love of his life, and he also began to withdraw from his family's social affairs. In spite of the animosity towards Gia from Dre's family, her family accepted Dre with open arms. Gia's brother Lil Rome was more focused with his music career and, he had a second hit song that was gaining popularity.

Dre thought it would be a good idea to shoot another video for Lil Rome's new song. The song was a catchy club hit, and Gia was featured on the chorus of the song. Unlike the first video, when Gia and Dre worked as a team to produce it. The production for this video was controlled solely by Dre. He wanted to film the video at a strip club and feature girls from the club in the video. Lil Rome really did not care how the video was produced, but Gia had immediate reservations about Dre and his video concept. Dre had set up the video shoot rather quickly and when it was time to film, Gia was not included. Even though she was featured on the song, Dre was going to have other girls ad lib her parts. Dre had made arrangements to film the video during the day when the strip club was closed, and Gia was conveniently at work. Gia was not happy about the fact that she was not featured in her brother's video, but she let Dre do what he thought was best. The evening after the video had been filmed and Gia was off work, Dre told her that he needed to go back to the club and get some extra footage. Gia thought this was odd, but she did not stop him from returning to the club. As it got later into the night, Dre had not returned from the strip club. Gia called Dre, but did not get an answer. Her intuition told her to go to the strip club and see what was really going on. Gia arrived at the club and Dre's car was in the parking lot. She called Dre on his cell phone again, and he still did not answer. Her next move was to go inside the strip club and see what the hell her man was doing, that was keeping him from answering his phone and coming home. Gia paid the cover charge and entered the dimly lit, loud club. She did not see Dre immediately so she sat at the bar and ordered a club soda. After two songs had been played by the DJ, Gia had scanned the entire club and still no Dre. She was frustrated and confused, where was Dre? Just as the DJ began to play the next song she heard Dre's laugh.

Gia looked in the direction where the laugh was coming from and what did she see! Coming out of the room clearly marked, *Dancers Only*, was Dre with two strippers. Gia was infuriated. One of the girls had her arm clearly wrapped around him. The other girl was adjusting her clothes as she walked with them. In the dimly lit club Gia could clearly see moisture on Dre's face that was being reflected from the light. Gia wanted to take her glass of club soda and smash one of the strippers in the face. Then a sudden calm overcame her, "Fuck them bitches, they are just some whores doing they job". Gia thought. Dre was the one in the wrong. Dre was the one who should be at home. Dre is the one that is supposed to care about her.

Gia exited the club without Dre noticing her and went directly to the parking lot. She looked at Dre's car, and like a bright star in the night, she noticed the perfect brick in the parking lot. Gia picked up the brick and did not hesitate to proceed to break every window in Dre's car. She broke the windows so quickly and without being noticed by club security, she decided to raise the stakes. Giovanna always kept a sharp knife in her vehicle. It was only natural that she got her knife and deliberately flattened all of the tires on Dre's vehicle. Now security had noticed her, but strangely they did not approach her or try to stop her. Gia drove home with a feeling of satisfaction of what she had done. She stopped at a convenience store to buy some chips and get some green tea, when her cell phone rang. "What the hell is wrong with you? Security said a woman in a fur coat had killed my car and I know it was you!" Dre said excitedly on the phone. Gia responded calmly, "You're right it was me." "Why did you fuck my car up?" Dre demanded. Gia again responded calmly, "Why are you not at home, in bed? Why were you hugged up with two bitches walking out of the dressing room?" Dre unconvincingly denied the accusations. "I don't know what you are talking about Gia. I told you I wanted to get some extra video footage.

It took a little longer than I thought, but I was coming home". Gia chastised Dre, "You were coming home, but you weren't home! I trusted you Dre, but I see you are just gonna do what you wanna do". Gia hung up on Dre and turned her phone off.

A crowd had gathered in the parking lot, and Dre's destroyed vehicle was the main attraction. His car was immobilized so he called a tow truck. Dre was now stranded at the strip club and Gia wasn't answering her phone. Dre went back into the strip club and drank heavily until the club closed. The manager called a cab for the inebriated Dre, and he spent the night at a motel alone. The next morning Dre continuously tried to call Gia unsuccessfully. His cousin, Big Slim, gave him a ride from the motel to his house. During the ride he explained his situation to his cousin, seeking some advice. "I really fucked up with Gia cuz. She came to the strip club and saw me with two bitches. I didn't see her but she was there and saw me". Dre explained. In an attempt to advise Dre, Big Slim added, "Cuz, just tell her the truth. You got drunk and you lost track of time. Were you getting a lap dance from those bitches"? Dre looked at his cousin with a guilty expression, "Naw I didn't get a lap dance, but I had a couple of them bitches compete in a dick sucking contest on me." Big Slim looked at Dre and simply responded, "Wow. Who won?" Dre laughed and said, "Not me." When they arrived at Dre's house Giovanna's car was not there. Big Slim let his cousin know that he could count on him if he needs him. The support of his family did not make Dre feel any better.

When Dre went into his house, he could smell the aroma of Gia's sweet perfume. He went to his bedroom, so that he could change out of the clothes he had been wearing since the day before. As Dre sat on his bed and began to get undressed, he noticed a piece of paper with his name handwritten on it, on his nightstand. It was a note from Giovanna that read: *To Dre, I hope you had fun doing whatever you were doing at the strip club. You are a grown man, and I can't stop you from doing what you want to do. If you choose to go to the strip club and be around those hoes, and you have me at home, I can't stop you. Don't wait up for me tonight. I'm going out with some of my girlfriends. I need a night for me, to clear my head and do me for a night. Don't worry, I'll be home. The kids are with my mother. I left you something to eat in the refrigerator. From, Gia.* Dre felt an empty feeling in his stomach. He was at home alone and powerless to do anything about how he had upset his beloved Gia. Dre walked to the liquor store, bought himself a pint of Vodka, and proceeded to drink and smoke his pain away.

Giovanna was utterly disgusted with Dre. When he never came home from the strip club, she figured that if Dre was doing him, she would do her. Gia made arrangements with her mother to take care of the kids. Gia also called a couple of her childhood friends, which she hasn't had a chance to hang out with lately. Gia had planned on going out with her friends, but decided a night out alone is what she needed. She went back home, not caring if Dre was there or not, her plans weren't going to change. Dre still wasn't at home so she got dressed, in hopes that she would be gone before he arrived. Gia got dressed in the shortest, skin tight mini skirt she could find in her closet. She paired that with a revealing top and some of new stiletto heels she had wanted to wear, but never have. She curled her long locks of hair and sprayed on some brand new perfume Dre had bought her for Mother's Day. Gia really did not have a destination, she just did not want to be in Dre's house or be around Dre.

While cruising through one of St. Louis's upscale entertainment districts, Gia was listening to the radio and heard a promo for a party that sounded like it would be fun. Gia headed to the club, when she arrived there were a lot of cars and a line of people waiting to get in the club. Gia valet parked her car and was about to get in line, when the doorman at the club told her that she did not have to wait in line with everyone else. Gia smiled and thanked him. This was the beginning of a night, where Gia would be the center of attention, for most of the men and some women at the club. Gia went to the bar to order a glass of champagne. As she attempted to pay for her drink, the man next to her offered to pay for her drink and told the bartender that whatever she ordered to put on his tab for the entire evening. The tall dark man looked at Gia said to her, "You are too damn fine to be paying for your own drinks. My name is Taylor. Get whatever you want and put it on my tab, but you gotta save me one slow dance and one crunk dance tonight." Gia smiled at her new friend, whom she thought resembled singer Tyrese, and agreed to his suggestion.

Giovanna loved to dance, and tonight she was gonna dance the night away. She followed her glass of champagne with a couple of tequila shots. The tequila numbed any guilt she may have had about the revealing outfit she was wearing. Gia wanted to dress sultry, but still sexy and classy. Guys were lining up to dance with Gia all night. The club had a stripper pole and she even found herself doing some pole dancing. When Gia was on the pole, a very sexy Filipino looking girl danced with her for a few songs. Gia was not bisexual, but she was feeling an attraction to her female dance partner. The girl introduced herself to Gia, "Hi, I'm Jasmine. You are one sexy mami! What is your name?" Gia was intrigued by Jasmine's advances. "My name is Giovanna, nice to meet you." Gia and Jasmine danced together for several songs, while most of the men in the club gazed at the two exotic women. Jasmine clung to Gia for the remainder of the evening. When Gia went to the restroom Jasmine followed. Every time Gia went to the bar, Jasmine was at her side. Gia had lost track of how many drinks she had that evening, and she did not care. Taylor had approached Gia and asked when he could have his dance. While they were talking, Jasmine looked at the two with a jealous eye and one of Gia's favorite songs came on. Gia grabbed Taylor by the hand and said, "C'mon this is my shit." Gia and Taylor went to the center of the dance floor and she danced erotically with him, while the music pumped through the speakers of the club. Taylor told Gia, "Damn girl, you really got it going on. Who are you here with?" Gia told him, "I'm with myself." Taylor asked, "I thought you were with that other girl I saw you hanging with all night." Gia replied, "Naw, I just met her in here." Another song came on and Gia and Taylor continued to dance. "What are you doing after the club?" Taylor asked Gia. "Whatever I want!" Gia quickly snapped. "You should holler at me before you leave. Maybe we can grab something to eat after the club." Taylor suggested. "We will see. I'll get back at you before I leave." Gia told him. As soon as Gia and Taylor stopped dancing, she felt someone grab her hand. It was Jasmine, and she was smiling slyly at Gia. "Who was that baby?" Jasmine asked

74

Giovanna. "Some guy I met at the bar." Gia replied. "He was all up on you mami. I thought I was going to have to grab you away from him." Jasmine said to Gia. Gia gave Jasmine a side-eyed look, and just smiled at her jealous new friend. Gia suggested that she and Jasmine have a shot of tequila, after the last call for alcohol was announced.

The club was closing and Jasmine was still clinging onto Giovanna. "Where are we going mami?" Jasmine inquired. "I'm not sure." Giovanna responded. As the two of them walked out of the club, Giovanna scanned to club to find Taylor. She had seen him all night, but he disappeared as the night got later. When Gia was walking out of the club, there was white on white Mercedes s550 parked in front of the club. Whoever was in the car began honking the horn and Gia faintly heard, "It's me Taylor." Gia walked towards the shiny vehicle, with Jasmine close behind, looked inside and she saw that it was the guy from the bar, Taylor. "I never asked you your name." A smiling Taylor said to Gia. Gia responded, "My name is Giovanna." Taylor then asked, "Are you hungry? We can go get something to eat, if you want." Gia pointed in the direction where her car was parked, and told Taylor to meet her near there. As Taylor pulled away, a jealous Jasmine was looking confused at Gia. "Well I see you got plans mami. Take my number, I would love to go out and dance with you again." Jasmine told Gia.

They exchanged phone numbers, and the two ladies went their separate way.

Gia walked to her car, and Taylor asked if she would like to ride with him. Gia was aware of how much she had been drinking, so she did not want to put herself in a bad situation with a strange man. Gia politely refused Taylor's offer, and told him to follow her to a place she liked. When Gia and Taylor arrived at the late night breakfast restaurant, they talked for a short time in the parking lot, before they went inside to eat. Gia took a few bites of her food, while Taylor cleaned his plate. This was the first time that Dre had crossed her mind all night. She was drunk, scantily dressed, and having breakfast with a guy she just met at the club. The frustration and anger with Dre she felt, returned. Gia looked at Taylor, who was physically totally opposite of Dre. She asked him bluntly, "So what are you trying to do tonight." Taylor was not immediately prepared to responds to Gia's question. He pondered what she had asked and replied, "I would like to do you tonight." Gia asked him if the seats in his car were heated. He confirmed that they were, and she told him to take her to his car. When Gia and Taylor got into his car, Gia reclined the passenger seat as far as it would go. She raised her short skirt up and asked Taylor, "Are you a good pussy eater?" An excited Taylor eagerly responded, "I can touch my nose with my tongue, and

76

breathe through my ears." A drunken Gia slid off her satin thong panties and told him to go to work. Taylor licked and sucked Gia's pussy, like a professional. Gia considered having sex with Taylor but noticed that he was masturbating while performing oral sex on her. After about 15 minutes of this spontaneous moment in the front seat of Taylor's car, Gia heard him moan and groan like he was about to orgasm. The weird and strange moment, sobered Gia up some. She observed Taylor achieve orgasm by masturbating himself, and she was immediately turned off by his selfish actions. "What if I wanted some dick, this nigga done already busted a nut." Gia thought to herself. Gia gathered herself, put her panties back on and told Taylor she had to go. An obviously infatuated Taylor asked Gia when they could hook up again. As Gia exited his car she told the starry eyed Taylor, "I'll call you". Gia drove home, thinking about the night she had. She did not have any feelings of guilt, but she did feel resentment towards Dre for pushing her over the edge, and behaving out of her normal character. When Gia got home, she saw Dre sleeping on the couch. Vodka and beer bottles on the floor and several blunt roaches in the ashtray. She didn't wake Dre. Gia took a shower, put on some sleeping clothes and got into her bed, alone.

Chapter Ten: "Break up to make up"

. Dre awoke out of his drunken stupor to find Giovanna sleeping peacefully in their bed. He noticed her sexy outfit strewn about the floor and wondered what she had been doing all night. Time had passed and the couple coexisted in the same house with minimal interaction. Gia focused on her work and herself, while Dre focused on his business and a video release party for Rome. It was an awkward time in their lives but when it was time for Rome's video release party, the couple would be forced to show a united front for the public.

The night of the premiere of Rome's video was going well for Gia and Dre. Gia was working at the front door, and Dre was working the crowd. They worked well together at public events. There was no indication that Gia and Dre were at a bad point in their lives, from the outside looking in. Throughout the night they made small talk with each other, interacted with mutual friends, and posed for several photos together. The evening in public together was actually therapeutic for Gia and Dre's relationship. They shared smiles and laughs which have been dormant for several weeks. When it was time to showcase the new video, the couple even held hands in anticipation of the viewing. Gia joked with Dre during the video, "Those bitches you got filling in for me on the song don't look as good as I do". Dre smiled at Gia and agreed. After the video was shown and the party resumed, there was an unexpected disturbance near the restrooms. Security responded and Dre followed to see what was happening.

Security was in the process of breaking up the confrontation near the restrooms and Dre saw that his cousin Smooth was involved. Smooth was arguing with a female and the distraught woman had created a tense scene with her loud talking and cursing. As security separated the two of them, a man that was obviously with the female hit Smooth in the back of the head with a beer bottle, a melee ensued. The female was with a group of people, and they swarmed on Smooth. They were punching him, kicking him, and throwing more beer bottles at him. Dre and Rome attempted to help his cousin by pulling people off of him while security unsuccessfully tried to regain control of the situation. It appeared that the brawl was about to get completely out of control, when additional confrontations began to erupt. The club owner however, knew exactly what to do to regain control his club. The owner of the club took his .38 revolver and fired two warning shoots into the ceiling. With the loud clap of gunfire, the crowd at the club quickly dispersed. Gia was hid safely behind the bar, with the money she made at the door. When the club had cleared out, she saw Dre and a bloodied Smooth. Fearing the worst Gia cried out, "Dre, are you alright?" Dre acknowledged that he was. "Smooth needs to go to the hospital." Dre yelled to her. The club owner was not happy with what had transpired at Dre's event. He told Dre, "Get your people some help, and you come see me tomorrow." Dre was not worried about the club owner. He just wanted to help his cousin that was bleeding profusely from his head.

An always calm Smooth thanked Dre for having his back. "Thanks man, I was getting rushed from so many directions I thought the entire club was jumping on me." A female that had remained inside the club during the confusion offered to take Smooth to the hospital. "Do you need someone to take you to the hospital to get checked out?" The unknown female asked. "I'm going to have her take me to get checked out. You and Gia get yourselves home. I will be alright", said a now smiling Smooth. Dre asked Smooth if he was sure and his cousin reassured him that he would be okay. His new lady friend was going to help nurse him back to health. Dre and Gia watched as Smooth acquainted himself with his new friend. "Your cousin is a trip", said Gia. Dre replied, "I know. He just got his ass beat and he still finds a way to meet a new female."

Gia, Rome, and Dre left the ransacked club. As they left Gia told Dre that despite all that had happened, it was a great night for business.

"I don't know how much the club owner made at the bar, but we did well at the door." Gia told Dre. Dre was obviously fatigued from the action he endured that night. He dropped off Rome, and then he and Gia began the ride home. "You seem like you are in good spirits tonight?" Dre said to Gia. "Hell yeah, the money was flowing through that door like a river, until the fight broke out. I even took a couple of people's money after the fight started." An ecstatic Giovanna told Dre. "I ain't mad at cha girl. You are always about you business." Dre replied. Gia continued, "That's why you love me Dre". Dre looked at her smiled and said, "You are right. One of the reasons I do love you is because you don't play about getting money." When they arrived at their house Gia suggested they wind down their exciting evening by watching a movie together. "I'm not tired. All of that action kind of has me hyped", Gia told Dre. As the two of them sat down and began to watch the movie while eating some microwave popcorn, Gia interjected. "Dre, I'm tired of all this silence around the house. Let's get everything that has happened with us out in the open." Dre looked at Gia and asked, "What's on your mind"? Gia asked him point blank, "What did you do with those two strippers at the strip club? Don't lie, because I know you did something." Dre reluctantly told Gia, "Well, I had them perform a blowjob contest on me." Gia looked disgustingly at Dre and stated, "Oh yeah, so that's what you was doing with those bitches? Why did you feel the need to do that Dre? I don't suck your dick well enough?" Dre responded, "You suck my dick great baby! I was drunk and I was on some bullshit." Gia countered, "You can't blame every mistake you make on, being drunk. You gotta man up, and take responsibility for the bullshit you put me through Dre." Dre agreed with Gia. Gia looked at Dre and debated whether she should tell Dre about what she had done with Taylor. "If he doesn't ask, I'm not about to volunteer anything", Gia thought to herself. Dre looked at Gia and thought to himself, "She said she wanted to get everything in the open. This is the perfect opportunity to ask her about her night out". Dre proceeded to ask Gia, "I saw the sexy outfit you had left on the floor. Where did you wear that outfit?" Gia responded, "I went to the club". Not fully satisfied with the information Dre continued his interrogation, "Who did you go to the club with?" Gia again responded, "I went by myself." Dre felt like whatever he was trying to get Gia to say, was not going to happen. He ended his questions, smiled at Gia, kissed her on her forehead and resumed watching the movie. Gia thought to herself, "If he asked the right question, she would not lie about what she had done with Taylor". Gia and Dre fell asleep on the sofa cuddled together while watching the movie.

Early that next morning, asleep on the sofa, Dre was awakened to Gia performing oral sex on him. Still groggy and a bit disoriented, Dre began to focus on what was happening to him. When Gia noticed that Dre was now awake to what she was doing she said to him, "I want you to tell me if whoever won your dicksucking contest sucked your dick better than me." Gia proceeded to perform the most incredible oral sex on Dre, which he could ever imagine. Dre could not believe how Gia did what she did with her mouth and tongue that it almost brought him to tears. As his toes curled and he moaned as he released his orgasm into Gia's welcoming mouth, Dre looked at Gia explained, "I have never experienced anything like that! Where did that come from?" Gia looked at Dre and told him, "I have a lot of talents. I can't show you everything at once. I gotta keep some until it is the right time to share them with you". Dre then told Giovanna, "I feel like I owe you something. I know what I can do for you baby, get on this couch and bend over for me." Gia followed his directions and when she was in the position Dre wanted, he proceeded to spread her ass cheeks and bury his face into her from behind. Gia was startled by what was happening to her, she had thought Dre was going to make love to her doggie style. He had never eaten her pussy from behind before, and she loved what he was doing to her. Dre made his tongue dive so deep into Giovanna that it took her breath away. He licked her vagina and gently sucked on her clitoris until her body began to tremble. Dre had plunged his face into her vagina for so long, Gia wondered if he would suffocate. As Dre sucked and licked while also penetrating her with his tongue Gia felt her body release an intense orgasm and she collapsed on the couch in ecstasy. Dre looked at Gia, his face covered with her wetness, and said, "I don't know who the best person to ever eat your pussy was, but I went for the crown today". Gia looked back at Dre and told him, "Nobody has ever done me like that daddy." They smiled, gave each other a loving hug, and got themselves together before one of their kids caught them being intimate on the living room sofa.

Gia and Dre had once again reconciled and reunited. It did not matter how many heart aches or heart breaks the couple shared, their love always endured. They loved each other, could not live without each other, depended on each other, Gia and Dre were made for each other. The time had passed and Gia's lease on her townhouse was almost ready to expire. There were several instances when Gia felt she was going to need to use her residential insurance policy, if living with Dre did not work. It was a roller coaster ride, but Gia endured. Her relationship with Dre was as strong and secure as it had ever been. She considered extending her lease six more months. In the back of her mind, she knew that Dre could potentially do something unpredictable to rock their steady union.

In the midst of this blissful period of their relationship, the company where Gia worked had announced layoffs. There was suddenly a sense of urgency of what Gia was going to do with her townhouse. If she was laid off of her job, she would not be able to afford to keep her own place. When it was finally apparent that she was going to be laid off from her job, Gia decided to let her townhouse lease expire. Now she was completely invested in her living arrangements with Dre. Dre made the situation of losing her job, easy for Giovanna. Nothing in her life had changed significantly. They still did everything they had always done. Though, Gia missed having her regular income. She received unemployment benefits, but that was far beneath what she was accustomed. Dre enjoyed having Gia at home. Dre kind of had old-school traditional male beliefs, that he did not want his woman to work. However being in a relationship with an independent minded woman such as Giovanna, he adjusted his beliefs. Dre even jokingly offered to give Gia an allowance if she stayed at home with the kids, instead of finding another job. This was not an option for Gia. She had always worked and always would work. It did not take long for Gia to find new employment. An international income tax company had offered Gia a position that was acceptable to her standards. When Gia had begun work at her new job, Dre was supportive and excited for her. They ate lunch together daily, and Dre often drove her to and from her new job. Dre admired the woman that Gia had become. She was no longer the single teenaged-mother, which worked at the strip club when he first met her. She was now an independent minded, confident, successful woman rubbing elbows in corporate America. Gia was not only hard-working, but also loving, considerate, dedicated, generous, and fully committed to him. Dre began to look at the love of his life, Giovanna, as more than the girlfriend he loved. He saw Giovanna as the woman he would like to spend the rest of his life with. Dre was starting to believe that Giovanna was the woman he would one day call, his wife.

Chapter Eleven: "The big question"

Gia and Dre were settled into a loving, deeply committed relationship with each other. The only difference between their relationship and a married couple was the marriage license and wedding rings. Dre thought he wanted to spend the rest of his life with Gia. Gia knew that she wanted to spend the rest of her life with Dre. Dre had already experienced an unsuccessful marriage. That experience left him with a bitter attitude about marriage. However, his relationship with Gia was totally different from his previous relationship with his ex-wife. Gia had always wanted a dream wedding, with her dream man. Like most women, from the time they were little girls and read about Cinderella, that dream relationship with Prince Charming is what every girl wanted. Dre wanted to be Gia's, Prince Charming. He had been in a relationship with Giovanna for almost four years now. He felt that if he did not step up to the plate and eventually propose to Gia, like a real man, his relationship with her would have been in vain. Giovanna was the only woman he wanted in his life. She was also the perfect woman for him. His best friend had recently gotten married, and Dre felt that the time was soon at hand for him to pop the big question to Giovanna.

During this time when Dre was pondering marriage, Rome was offered an opportunity to promote his music in Texas. Texas was a huge market for independent rap and Dre knew that this was an excellent chance for them to expand Rome's fan base. Dre conferred with Gia about the music opportunity in Texas, and with her support they proceeded on a Texas road trip that included Dallas, Houston, and Austin. Rome's music was received well on the trip. Dre made numerous business contacts and the 5-day venture was more than successful. Dallas was the last city where they stopped. While in Dallas, Dre and Rome were finishing up their last piece of business at a music store, in a popular mall. When their business was complete and as they were ready to begin preparation for the trip back to St. Louis, Dre unexpectedly stopped at a jewelry store. Dre made a bee line directly to the engagement rings. Rome did not know what Dre's sudden detour was about. He saw him looking at engagement rings and assumed he knew what was transpiring. "Are you looking for an engagement ring bro?" Rome asked. Dre kept examining the rings in the case and nonchalantly replied, "Who me?" As Dre was responding to Rome, a beautiful engagement ring set in white gold, with an emerald-cut diamond center surrounded by baguette and round diamonds captured his eye. Dre asked for some assistance from the sales person at the jewelry store. "Tell me about this ring", Dre said to the sales person. As the sales person shared the details and price about the ring with him, a now excited Rome interrupted the sales pitch and asked Dre, "Are you about to ask Sissy to marry you?" Dre focused on the details about the ring, being described by the sales person and totally ignored Rome. When the sales person was finished with the pitch, Dre had only one question. "Can I pay for this ring with half on my credit card and the other half with cash?" Dre asked. The sales person smiled widely and replied, "Certainly sir". Rome was now also smiling widely and could not control his emotions any longer. "You are going to ask Sissy to marry you! I'm so happy for ya'll bro!" Rome hugged Dre, while the sales person took the ring to be boxed and gift wrapped. Dre looked at Rome and explained, "Yeah bro, I'm going to pop the big question. I have been with your sister for a long time, and she has put up with a lot of bullshit from me. If any woman can deal with me as long as your sister has, I know she is the woman that I want to spend the rest of my life with." Dre completed the engagement ring purchase, and he and Rome began the trip back to St. Louis.

"Now I don't need you to tell this to anybody! Don't say anything to your momma, your brother, your homies, hell don't even talk about this with me anymore". Dre told Rome as soon as they returned to St. Louis. "I'm not sure when or how I will ask your sister to marry me, and I don't want her to suspect anything." Dre explained. "I ain't saying shit bro. As a matter of fact, I don't even know what we are talking about right now." Rome reassured Dre. Dre dropped off Rome and headed home to reunite with Giovanna. "I missed you baby!" An excited Gia exclaimed to Dre as he walked into their house. She ran over towards him and they embraced and greeted each other with a passionate kiss. In anticipation of Dre's return home, Gia had prepared his favorite meal, lasagna. "Is that lasagna I smell?" A joyful Dre asked. "You know it baby." She replied. Dre relaxed and enjoyed his meal after the long road trip away from home. Dre and Gia retired to their bedroom where he told her all about the Texas trip with Rome. After the recap Dre also informed Gia, "My mother wants me to come over to her house and stay with my grandmother on Saturday. She is going out of town for the weekend. My sister is going to stay with her on Friday night, and she needs me to be there on Saturday." Gia offered to accompany Dre. "I haven't seen your grandmother in a long time. I miss her. She's the only person in your family that has always showed me genuine love. Do you mind if I come with you?" Dre replied, "I was hoping you would want to come." Dre continued, "I have an early morning studio session with Rome. We got some new beats from a producer we linked up with in Texas. This sound is different from anything we have ever recorded."

Always supportive, Gia stated, "I can't wait to hear the new tracks." Following Gia and Dre catching up with each other after time apart, the two of them drifted off into a relaxing slumber with the television on and cuddled close together.

At Rome's studio session that next morning, Dre had invited Big Slim and Smooth to attend. He wanted to invite his cousin CJ, but they had some creative differences and CJ had started his own group and record label. CJ had formed a group with one of Rome's main music producers. He even had financial backing by some Colombian that was supposed to be a drug kingpin. Dre still supported his cousin, CJ. They just no longer worked together on music. Dre had invited Big Slim and Smooth to the studio session so that he could share with them his plan of getting engaged to Gia. "Well fellas, I think I'm ready to turn in my players' card." Dre told them. "Check out this ring I picked up while we were in Texas." Dre then showed them the ring. "Man, I'm happy for you cuz." Big Slim immediately stated while admiring the ring. "Does this mean, time for a bachelor party?" Smooth added. "I'm not sure if I want to have a bachelor party, yet." Dre countered. "Well, just let me know and I will put together the bachelor party of the decade for you." Smooth insisted. "I'm so proud of you cuz, you and Gia will be great as husband and wife." Big Slim said. Dre continued, "Ya'll two are the first people I have told. I'm going to keep it traditional and ask her mom for her permission later on today." While Dre was breaking the news about his engagement plans, Rome was in the sound booth laying some hot tracks on his Texas beats. "Man, that shit ya'll got from Texas goes hard!" Big Slim exclaimed as he listened to the music being recorded. Smooth and Big Slim left the studio while Rome was still recording tracks. When the studio session had finished, Dre and Rome rode together to Gia's mother's house. "When we get to your house, I'm going to ask your mother for permission to marry Gia." Dre said to Rome. "I don't know what you are talking about bro." Rome replied. They both laughed as Rome sparked a blunt for the ride to his house.

When they arrived at Gia's mom's house, Dre found her in the kitchen. "Hey boo-boo!" Gia's mother said as she greeted Dre. "Hey mom", Dre responded. "Can I talk to you for a minute mom? I would like to ask you about something that is kind of serious." He added. Showing concern about the Dre's dilemma, she responded, "Sure boo-boo, you know you can talk to Mom about anything. What is bothering you?" Dre sat down with a blank expression on his face. He then let a smile through and stated, "I want to marry Giovanna, Mom. I love her and I want to spend the rest of my life with her. I just want your blessing, before I ask her." Gia's mother hugged Dre and with an elated response she said, "You don't have to ask for my blessings boo-boo. You have always been a son to me. I always told my pumpkin, that you two were going to have a lot of babies and ya'll were going to be together forever." Overjoyed with the response that Dre had gotten from Gia's mother, he gave her a big hug told her that he loved her and headed home in anticipation of Giovanna arriving from work.

When Gia arrived home, she noticed how playful Dre was. He also kept asking her random questions. "How many kids would you like to have with me? Do you think we would still like each other when we get old? Would you still love me if I were fat, bald and gray?" Gia figured he had smoked too much of his purple weed with Rome at the studio, and was tripping out. Dre was not sure where and when he wanted to ask Gia to marry him. He wanted it to be a total unexpected surprise. It was hard to surprise Giovanna, but Dre was determined to catch her off guard. He pondered the rest of the week, without an opportune moment to ask her. Then the Saturday, he was supposed to spend with his grandmother had arrived, and he thought that this might be his chance. Dre's grandmother suffered from dementia, and she could not be left home alone. Although her memory suffered, Dre's grandmother always knew who Giovanna was. Giovanna had a strong affection for Dre's grandmother, because unlike most of the other women in his family, she always kept it real. Dre's grandmother fell asleep early and he offered to warm up some leftover food while she slept. While they sat and ate the food Gia noticed the permanent smile that was on Dre's face. "What the hell are you smiling about?" She asked Dre. "I'm just smiling at you. I've been watching you show my grandmother so much love and attention all night. That's just another reason why I love you so much." Dre replied. "Well everybody in your family tries to act like your grandmother is crazy. She just knows that they are the one's that are crazy, not her." Gia stated. Gia began to wash the dishes they had just eaten on. Dre sat at the kitchen table watching her. He felt like this was the perfect time to put his heart on the table for Giovanna. Dre said a prayer, took a deep breath and walked over to Giovanna, while she was standing at the sink. He told her, "You don't have to wash the dishes baby. I'll take care of them." She quickly countered, "That's okay baby. I'll take care of these dishes. I don't want your momma to say I messed up her kitchen." Gia looked at Dre and he still had that permanent smile on his face. "What is wrong with you? Why are you smiling at me like that?" She asked him. Dre grabbed Gia by both of her hands. They were still wet with dishwater. He looked directly into her deep penetrating eyes and told her, "I love you Giovanna." She replied, "I love you too, Dre." He held her wet hands tighter and placed them upon his heaving chest and continued, "No, I REALLY LOVE YOU, Giovanna. I have never loved anyone the way I loved you baby." He proceeded to drop to one knee. Gia felt her heart begin to race and a big smile overtook her face when she saw what he was doing. "Giovanna, I love you more than life itself. I want to spend the rest of my life with you. Will you marry me baby?" Dre professed to her. Tears of joy began to form in Giovanna's beautiful eyes. She looked at the man she wanted, the man she would do anything for, the man that she loved more than she loved herself, on his knee asking her to spend the rest of her life with him. She had known she wanted to spend the rest of her life with Dre, the moment she first laid eyes on him. When times were hard, and her heart was hurting, there were times she doubted this moment would ever come. Without hesitation, Gia looked into the sincere and loving eyes of Dre and said, "Yes! Yes I will marry you Dre!"

Chapter Twelve: "Here we go again"

After nearly four years of dedication, love, heartbreak, happiness, separation, and reconciliation, Dre and Gia were now engaged to be married. Giovanna and Dre are two souls in love. Giovanna loves Dre more than she loves herself. Dre loves Giovanna more than life itself. Their story is about a love so strong, so intense, and so unyielding. Their relationship has taken them on a roller coaster ride of life. The bond between Giovanna and Dre has been tested by family, friends, and strangers alike. Temptation, jealousy, greed, and envy have tested the resilience of their love. In spite of everything that has so far entrenched upon the relationship of Giovanna and Dre, they remain deeply in love with each other. That is the only thing that ultimately matters to them. They have now decided they are ready to make a commitment to each other, for life. Gia and Dre believe there is nothing or no one can, that can break their unconditional love, undeniable desire, and unbridled passion that they have for each other.

Gia was excited about being a bride. She decided to plan the wedding herself, so that nothing would go overlooked on her big day. Dre was not as active in the wedding planning as Gia. He basically accommodated her every need and want for their wedding date. Gia loved the color pink, and that was going to be the main color theme for their nuptials. They are not a traditional couple, so Gia planned a non-traditional wedding. Instead of renting a church for the ceremony, Gia reserved a beautiful rose garden at a public park. Gia loved flowers and she thought that an outdoor ceremony in the rose garden would be very romantic. Gia did not want a lot of bridesmaids, so she asked four of her closest friends to all be her maids of honor. Her mother would cater the reception, and she would coordinate the invitations, music selections, and decorations herself. Gia handled the task of planning her wedding with ease.

Dre's excitement for the wedding was not as obvious as Gia's. He took a supportive role, with her planning for their big day. He was able to reserve a pink limo for his fiancé and he found a pink suit for the wedding. He had also chosen his cousin Big Slim as his best man. Dre might not have shown much excitement for his wedding, but he did seem to be looking forward to his bachelor party. His cousin Smooth had promised to throw Dre the bachelor party of the decade. Dre initially had reservations about hosting a bachelor party. However, Gia encouraged him to have one. So he decided to go ahead and have one last night out with the boys. The reality of being married was slowly setting into Dre's mind. He loved Gia, and he looked forward to starting a new chapter in his life. Dre knew he was truly a lucky man, for a woman like Gia to accept his marriage proposal.

The bachelor party was held the week before the wedding. Dre knew he was going to be drinking heavily at his party. That is why it was planned a week earlier, to avoid anyone having a hangover at the wedding ceremony. Smooth had rented a penthouse suite at one of St Louis' finest hotels. He had everything set up for a once in a lifetime bachelor party. The room was stocked with a bathtub full of liquor and beer. There was an ounce of pre-rolled blunts in the kitchenette and party platters of bar-b-q. Smooth spared no expense for his cousin's bachelor party. He booked four of his favorite dancers, to provide the entertainment for the evening. When Dre arrived at the party, he had already been drinking with Big Slim and Rome. Most of the invited guests were already at the party when they had arrived. When the groom was introduced to the female entertainment, they immediately sat him down and gave him a group erotic lap dance. This was the start of an unforgettable bachelor party.

Dre's bachelor party started off tame, but got wild quickly. The liquor was flowing, the weed was burning, and some lines of cocaine were consumed. The ladies that provided the entertainment were totally uninhibited. They provided a girl on girl sex show for the partygoers. The more money the guys made rain on the ladies, the more risqué the entertainment became. Rome was enjoying himself to the fullest. He had two girls give him a simultaneous lap dance, smoked plenty of weed, and drank tequila shots with his future brother-in-law. Rome was having the time of his life when he unexpectedly disappeared from the festivities. Big Slim, Smooth, and the rest of Dre's friends continued with the non-stop smoking and drinking at the bachelor party.

Dre noticed that Rome was missing and had set out to find him. After checking all of the rooms, he found Rome on the patio. "What's wrong bro? I was looking for you to see if everything was okay." Dre said when he found Rome. Rome exhaled smoke from the black and mild cigar he was smoking and told him, "I have to leave the party early bro. Some of my homies called, and they are coming to pick me up." Dre responded, "Fuck them man! Tell them that you are at my bachelor party, and you can't leave tonight!" Rome smiled and said, "It's all good bro. I didn't plan on staying all night any way. One of the homies is moving to Chicago and we are sending him off with a goodbye bar-b-q." Dre was disappointed that Rome had to leave early. While they were still on the patio, Rome's cell phone rang. After the call he told Dre, "Well bro, the homies are here. Kick it hard for me bro." Dre told

99

Rome, "If you want to come back, we are going to be here all night. I'll have someone pick you up if you need a ride." Rome replied, "It's all good bro. I'll call you if I need you. I'm so happy for you and Sissy. I always knew ya'll would be together forever. I love you bro." Rome gave Dre some dap and a hug. Dre walked with Rome to meet his homies and he waved goodbye to Rome, as he watched him ride away in the backseat of the car.

Dre returned to the party to see that everyone had stripped to just their underwear. An intoxicated and excited Smooth put his arm around Dre and told him, "I told all of the squares to leave, because for the rest of the night we are partying in just our drawers." Dre got with the new theme of the party and immediately took off his shirt and pants. The girls had taken a break while Smooth filtered out all of the party guests that did not want to stay at the underwear only bachelor party. Once the festivities resumed, the girls announced that if anyone wanted a blowjob, the head doctor would be taking care of patients in the upstairs bathroom. Several of the fellas immediately headed towards the bathroom, while the remaining girls worked the crowd of men. All was going well at the party, until one of the girls sprayed whip cream on Dre. He did not want any type of flavor or sticky substance on him and the whip cream had put a damper on his mood. Smooth sensed the tension and came up with an instant solution. Only Smooth would suggest that the girls clean up the mess they made on Dre. "Hey ladies, the groom can't get anything on him tonight. Since ya'll got whip cream on him, now he needs to be cleaned up." Smooth had announced to the ladies. Two of the girls told Dre that they would gladly clean him up. They escorted him to the shower, removed his remaining clothes and both of them soaped him up and scrubbed him from head to toe. The crowd of partiers began cheering loudly for Dre because he was being bathed by two naked strippers in the shower. Dre obviously enjoyed the treatment he was getting, as he decided to return the favor and scrub down the two strippers in the shower with him.

After the shower scene, the party turned up even more. One of the girls unveiled some sex toys and let various partiers use them on her. Another girl disappeared to a bedroom, where several men at the party had sex with her. Some of the intoxicated guests passed out from drinking too much, others could not control their liquor and had to be sent home in taxicabs. By the time the sun had begun to rise, the wild party was finally coming to an end. Dre had to leave in haste, because he promised Gia he would be home before sunrise. Smooth, Big Slim, and a few others chose to hang out until it was time to check out of the suite. "Cuz, I appreciate everything you did for my party, but it's time for me to get home." Dre told Smooth before he left the hotel room. Smooth then told Dre, "This night was just for us. We are going to keep everything that happened last night between us. Last night never happened." Smooth and Dre shook hands and Dre left what was remaining of the party. Dre drove home feeling slightly guilty about what he did in the shower at his bachelor party. He was also thinking about the fact that Gia would probably cancel the wedding if she knew what he did at his bachelor party. Dre locked the events of his bachelor party in the back of his mind, never to be revealed or spoken about again. The bachelor party happened, but it didn't happen in Dre's mind.

When Dre returned home, Gia was sleeping soundly in their bed. Dre was hung over and felt a bit sick, so he went to the bathroom as a precaution. While he was in the bathroom his cell phone rang. "Who the hell is calling me this early in the morning?" Dre thought to himself. He did not recognize the number on his caller ID, so he ignored the call. His cell phone rang again and it was the same unknown number. Dre wondered to himself, "Did I give my number to one of the strippers? Did something happen after I left the hotel? Who the hell is calling me, this early in the morning?" Dre again ignored the call. His cell phone rang yet again, and Dre finally answered. "Dre, this is Pook. I got something to tell you cuz." The voice on the other line had said to Dre.

Dre gathered his thoughts and realized Pook was one of Rome's friends. "What's up Pook?" Dre replied. "Dre, I hate to have to tell you this, but Rome got shot." Pook informed Dre. Dre was listening to what Pook had just told him, but he wasn't sure of what he heard Pook say. "What did you just say?" Dre asked Pook. Pook responded quickly, "Rome got shot last night. He lost a lot of blood and we had to rush him to the emergency room." Dre heard Pook, but still wasn't grasping what he was being told. Gia then interrupted the conversation, "Hey baby. Who keeps calling your phone?" Dre just told her, "It's Pook." Gia then asked, "What does he want with you?" Dre then told Pook, "Man, it's too early in the morning to be playing on the phone." Pook interrupted Dre, "I'm not playing cuz. Rome is at the hospital, in critical condition, and they are not sure if he is going to make it." Dre finally comprehended what he was being told. "He is at Martin Luther King hospital. I'm sorry Dre, we did all we could to help Rome." Pook confessed. Gia was in the bathroom with Dre and could see the solemn expression on his face. She immediately asked, "What is wrong with my brother?" Dre thanked Pook for calling him, and looked at Gia. She already had a look of distress and again asked Dre, "What happened to my brother? Pook would not be calling you this early unless something was wrong with my brother." Dre hesitated, looked at Gia and gave her a hug. She immediately broke into tears as Dre told her, "Rome got shot last night and is in critical condition at Martin Luther King." Gia fell to her knees and cried aloud. Dre tried to console his grief stricken fiancé. A devastated Giovanna kept saying out loud, "I told my brother about hanging with those niggas. I told my brother about hanging with those niggas." Dre was in complete disbelief about what he was just told. Gia unconsciously got herself dressed and headed straight for the car, leaving Dre behind. Dre hurriedly caught up with Gia at her car and they sped to the hospital where Rome was.

When they arrived upon the chaotic scene at the hospital emergency room entrance, they saw one of Rome's friends being questioned by police detectives. The backseat of the same car Dre saw Rome leave his bachelor party, was now soaked with blood and a blood trail led into the hospital emergency entrance. Gia saw all of the blood and said, "I know that's my brother's blood." Rome's friend that was being questioned by the police looked at Gia and Dre and hung his head in shame. Gia ran into the hospital with Dre close behind and demanded to see her brother. "Where is my brother? Where is my brother? I need to see my brother!" She demanded. A nurse tried unsuccessfully to get Gia to remain calm. Then a doctor in scrubs came to the nurse's assistance and told Gia, "We are working hard to keep your brother with us. He lost a lot of blood, but he has a pulse again." An unusual calm came over Gia and she said to the doctor, "He has a pulse again." The doctor responded, "Yes, he flat lined soon after he arrived, but we brought him back." Gia's legs got weak and Dre helped her to a chair. The doctor returned to the operating room while Gia and Dre sat in the waiting room devastated from what they just learned about Rome. After a few minutes of sitting, a social worker approached them and asked them come with her to a private room. When they entered the private room, the social worker informed them that she was going to have a priest come and sit with them. Gia heard this and thought the worse about Rome, "My brother is dead! Why else would they send a priest to sit with us?" Dre wrapped his jacket around Gia while they waited for the priest. They sat together in the private room at the hospital, and began to pray feverishly for Rome. Gia and Dre fell to their knees and prayed and prayed and prayed for Rome. Gia felt like her world was coming to an end. She loved her little brother Rome dearly. She did not know how she would go on with her life, without her brother being a part of it. The last thing she was ready to accept was the death of her brother.

When she and Dre got up, to sit back down from praying, she nonchalantly places her hands into the pockets of Dre's jacket. She thought she felt something to wipe her tears away, but what she pulled out of the jacket was some female underwear that did not belong to her. Dre had seen what Gia pulled out of his jacket and recognized the panties from one of the strippers at his bachelor party. Dre thought to himself, "Was I that drunk that I kept some panties from the bachelor party." Gia looked at Dre and told him, "These do not belong to me." Dre had a confused, guilt ridden expression on his face, and said, "I don't know where those came from." Gia looked at Dre with sadness and disgust. She thought to herself, "Did this nigga really have some bitches' panties in his jacket?" Giovanna calmly threw the panties in the trash and sat back down next to Dre. She then looked at Dre and asked, "Really Dre? You keeping bitches panties now?" Dre did not respond to Gia. He did not know how to respond to Gia. The only thing that raced through his mind was the fact that he was supposed to get married in a week and his fiancé just found a pair of strange panties in his jacket. Before Dre could respond to Gia, the doctor, social worker, and priest entered the room where they were waiting. The doctor and social worker sat down and the priest said, "I would like to pray with you about your brother Rome."

The love saga of Giovanna and Dre continues in the new novel

"Good Girls Finish Last"

By Ben E. Lewis & Luciana Santiago

Follow on twitter:
@benlewkc
@MzSantiago

Now available

"Gangsta-Gangsta"

By Ben E. Lewis

Made in the USA
San Bernardino, CA
24 September 2014